THE CHEATING HUSBAND

A Psychological Thriller

James Caine

Twisted Thriller Books

PROLOGUE

When I see the couple on the bed, their vacant eyes staring off into nothing, I'm not so sure if this was truly what I wanted. This wasn't what I planned.

It's one thing to think about murder. It's another to strategize about how to do it and not get caught. And it's the ultimate level to take it beyond planning and actually commit it. But this was what I wanted. Blood. Death. Murder. Justice. My revenge.

Cheater's justice.

I fight back the tears, but a few squeeze past my eyelids. If this is what I wanted, why am I sad?

This isn't what I planned for, not exactly. I was so meticulous on how I wanted tonight to go, but nothing went the way it was supposed to.

The dead couple are arranged on the bed, their limbs placed around each other. Quite a beautiful pair they make, even in death. Ruining the moment are the etched expressions of fear their faces managed to contort into in their last living moments.

The image sticks with me more than I thought it

would.

I stare at their bare chests, leaning over the bed to examine the heart symbol that's etched into them. A large X is crossed over each.

The Heartbreak Killer is back.

I take a deep breath and look at the nightstand beside the bed. On it is a bloody box cutter. On the other nightstand is something worse. Something else I didn't plan for. I realize instantly what went wrong.

I look at the dead stares of the couple and lower my head. If this is what I wanted, why are the tears still streaming down my face? I'm more than confused.

Realizing I shouldn't stay here much longer, I take a deep breath to compose myself. Now is not the time to ruminate. I need to leave.

My daughter is still at my father's house. I need to get back to him quickly. I need to establish my alibi. I need to compose myself, now more than ever, to not make any mistakes.

A loud bang on the front door startles me. "Police! Open the door!" The banging gets louder as my eyes widen.

The police are here. How? It's not possible. Who called them?

"Open the door!" the deep voice of the officer bellows. I'm not able to respond. Instead, I freeze, staring at the bodies on the bed.

This is not what I planned.

CHAPTER 1

Emma

"You always have a home with me, Emma. Don't forget that," my sister Julie says in her usual warm but condescending tone. It's one that screams: You should just come back to my house. What you're doing isn't working, and you're going to fail anyway, so just come back and save yourself from the embarrassment of being you.

My sister likes to pretend she's much older and wiser than me despite being only nine months my senior. As grateful as I was when I lived with her the past few years, I'd love nothing more than to shout at her that it's nobody's dream to live in their sister's semi-developed basement.

"Thanks," I say instead, holding my cell away from my lips for a brief moment to not let slip what I'm thinking.

Julie is the definition of a good sister. She truly is always there for me, no matter what. No matter what I've done or how I've messed up, she has my back. I love her for that, but sometimes I wish she'd just take a step back and let me make my own decisions without putting in her two cents.

"How's the job search going?" Julie continues.

I nearly sigh into the phone. When she called, initially I didn't want to answer. I was looking online for jobs, checking my emails to see if I got any responses to the resumes I put out. Nothing, though.

"It's going okay," I say, keeping it short.

"Mm," Julie mutters. I'm waiting for her to ask me how many resumes have I put out yesterday, or did I follow-up with any employers, or have I attended any career fairs. Windsor, Ontario may not be the biggest city, but there's plenty of work to be had if I truly want it.

"I'm trying, Julie," I say with a slight tone. "I am. It's not easy, okay?" I swear, my sister likes to pretend she's my mother. She may have her life put together, being married, with a decent job and having given me the cutest nephew ever, but I'm just not in the mood to feel kicked down today.

"I didn't say anything," Julie says innocently.

I sit on the couch in the living room and sigh. "I know, but I can feel your thoughts. They're all negative."

"I have a great idea, dear sister." Julie laughs. "Maybe you can get a job as a fortune teller since you already know what I'm going to say."

I don't need tarot cards or a crystal ball to see how the rest of the conversation will go. She'll make a bunch of subtle comments that suggest the only real plan in my life should be living in her basement out in the country.

A place where everything smells like manure all day and eligible bachelors are non-existent.

No thanks.

I did it for years. While living there was peaceful, and I loved spending time with my nephew, Rowan, city life suits me best. If I'm being honest with myself, I also hated living below someone who had the perfect life.

One I'd kill for.

A large house with a literal white picket fence surrounding their acreage. A forested area around their property to go on endless trail hikes and exploring. Even her husband is handsome. Despite putting on a few pounds and showing the early stages of balding at the back of his scalp, David's a good-looking man.

A decent man. A good father.

Faithful. You don't have to question whether David will be there for Julie. It's a given. He would do anything for her.

When I lived with them, David and I had this weird tension between us. When I reflect on it, I don't think it was anything he did. He could be a little stuck up sometimes. He'd like to mention that he's a doctor, and I'd throw it back that he's just a chiropractor. He laughed the first time I made that joke but found it less funny over time.

Sometimes I think I was upset at the idea of him. A dependable man that would be by your side. This type of man was a myth to me until recently.

For a long time, I thought a man like David was not

in my cards. Months ago, if I did have a crystal ball or had been a professional fortune teller, I'd likely have told you I'd be single forever.

That was until Owen Pearson came into my life.

Just thinking of him now makes me smile. I think that's why I picked up the phone call from Julie so confidently today. I'm ready to tell her about him, well, sort of.

"I'm just worried about you, Emma," my sister says, and I do hear the warmth in her voice as she says it. "Are you still living downtown?" She sighs. "Such a sketchy area. I want to visit you in the city, but it's just not safe."

I don't bother getting into that conversation again. She's going to tell me how crime-ridden the area is, and I'll tell her I can take care of myself. She'll say it's nice and clean and crime-free in Essex County. Instead of responding and engaging in a conversation I know will go bad, I change the subject.

"So, I'm seeing someone," I say, biting my lip.

My sister squeals. "Oh, now I need the details. Give me everything, sister."

"He's tall, dark and handsome, just how I like them."

Julie laughs. "So, does this mysterious tall dark and handsome man have a name?"

"I'll tell you someday," I say. It's superstitious I know, but it feels like anytime I tell my sister anything about my personal life that's going well, everything derails. It's almost as if telling her about something that makes me happy dooms it immediately.

Julie sighs. "Okay, so, is this a serious thing?"

"We've been seeing each other for nearly four months."

"Four months!" Julie shouts. "You haven't told me about your new man for that long? Plus you won't even give me a name!" She authentically sounds hurt.

"I just wanted to make sure things were real with him."

I don't have a good track record with men. Dating in general seems to be something I fail at every given chance.

"Don't give up on love," my mom would tell Julie and I when we were kids. Although our mother's marriage and life were a complete disaster, somehow my mom's enthusiasm for not giving up stuck with me.

With the number of terrible men I've been with, sometimes I question why I haven't given up yet.

"That's understandable," Julie says. "You seem to attract some *special* guys."

I laugh off her comment, but inside it stings. Julie has a way of being playful while having her words hurt with their realism.

"Well, tell me about the mystery man," she says. "What does he do?"

Why is that the first question she asks? It's not "tell me how you met" or "why you like him", but how much money he makes. What's his job title, so I can measure how much respect I should give him. I want to shove it in her face that Owen isn't a pretend doctor, like David, but bite my lip.

Thankfully, this time, I have a good answer that will satisfy even my sister's criticisms of the typical men I'm with.

"He's a real estate agent," I say.

"Oh," Julie says. "That's cool. Does he do well?" I can't help but sigh. "What?" Julie asks again. "I'm just curious."

"Well, Julie," I say playfully, "I'll have you know that he appears to be doing quite well in Windsor."

I put our call on speaker and look at a photo I took last month of the bus stop near my apartment. On the bench is an advertisement promoting Owen's real estate services, with him brandishing his handsome smile. "Your dream life starts with me," the ad says beside him. I always laugh when I see it, the irony of the words making my heart flutter, because it's true. Ever since he came into my life, my world feels perfect. I sent a picture of me sitting beside his face, waving my arms towards the words, to Owen as a joke.

Before I met him in person, I had seen the ad on the bench many times. I'd look at his gorgeous face and feel moved by him. Maybe it was the words his ad promised.

He seemed so put together in the ad in his navy suit. When I was going for a long walk along the riverside downtown, I ended up in an older neighborhood with most of the Victorian-styled houses built in the early

1900s.

In the front yard of one of the larger houses was a sale sign with Owen's face on it. It was the same image used in the bus stop ad. I was immediately intrigued. As if it was fate for us to meet, the words "Open House" were tacked at the top of the sign. Balloons were tied to the front door.

I couldn't help myself.

"I actually met him at an open house he had for one of his properties," I admit to Julie.

"You're looking for houses?" she says, confused.

I laugh. I mention how I saw an ad of him and gushed over it. "When I saw he was having an open house, I couldn't help myself. I needed to see him in real life."

"So, how was he in person? I take it that his image wasn't completely photoshopped if you're with him."

"Even better looking in person. He's something else. Maybe next time you come to the city you can meet him."

Julie whistles. "My sister wants me to meet her boyfriend?"

I laugh. "That's right." I'm just as shocked as she is.

"Well, hopefully if I do, you can let me in on what his name is." She laughs. "That would be great though. I don't even remember the last time I met a guy you were with." There's a brief pause. "Oh wait, I do! That gangly-looking guy. Aaron something."

I sigh. "Aaron Wiers."

She laughs again. "Right. More like Aaron Wires. He was so thin. And despite having the most awkward energy I've ever met in a man, he was the one who broke it off with you. Said he was moving to another province but then you see him in the city next month."

Somehow my sister always has a way of ruining my good news.

I hear the faint sound of my nephew in the background. "Is that Rowan?"

"It is," Julie says. "He wants to talk to you too."

She hands the phone over to my nephew, who doesn't say anything right away. He's only five, and even though he doesn't say a word, I can see his cute face smiling as he places the phone awkwardly to his ear as if I'm in the room with him.

"Rowan?" I say into my phone. "Are you there?"

There's a pause before he says, "Hey, Auntie," in his small, high-pitched voice. Hearing him speak always brightens my day.

"How are you, buddy?" I say. "I miss you. I hope I get to see you soon."

"I miss you too. Thank you for my toy."

"He loves his new toy truck!" Julie shouts in the background. "He can't stop playing with it since he got it."

"Aww," I say, my smile widening. "You're welcome, Rowan."

It's not just any toy truck. It's based on a truck called Gravedigger we saw at a monster truck show eight months ago. Rowan freaked out at the live event as the large truck smashed into smaller vehicles. He really wanted to buy a Gravedigger T-shirt but they didn't have any left in his size after the show.

"So you like your Gravedigger truck?" I ask. He starts making engine revving sounds, and I laugh.

"He keeps smashing into other toys with it, Emma!" my sister shouts.

There's another pause before Rowan says something. I can hear Julie whispering something to him.

"Mommy wants me to ask you when you are moving back here."

I laugh at my sister's desperation. "Have fun playing with your new toy, bud. You can put your mom back on."

"Bye, Auntie," Rowan says. I can hear him running off before Julie starts talking.

"He wasn't supposed to tell you I told him to say that," my sister says.

"Ha ha," I say, shaking my head. "I'm doing fine in Windsor, really. You'll see. Things are getting better. For once, I'm really excited."

There's a pause. "I'm happy for you," Julie says. I hear the faint sound of Rowan making engine sounds again. "Also, Rowan really does love that toy. It's not even his birthday or anything, so we were both surprised when he got it in the mail. He's been obsessed with it since."

I smile. "Well, a month ago, I heard him say how much he wanted to go back to the monster truck show. I wanted to get him something. A gift at an unexpected time is always so much better."

There's another pause. "What's wrong?" I ask.

"I know you're between jobs right now. You didn't have to buy him something."

I sigh. "I wanted to, Julie. I'm the aunt who gets to spoil their nephew. I have savings. I'll be fine."

"You shouldn't spend much more of your inheritance money. If you're struggling, you can—"

"Always come back to your house," I say.

She laughs. "Well, it's true. I'm sure that your mystery man wouldn't mind picking you up in the country for a date."

I turn on the television, sifting through the few channels I can get with an antenna. I'm not sure if it's to get away from my conversation with Julie or distance myself from my own feelings.

A local news show piques my interest immediately.

The anchor smiles for the camera as he shuffles a bunch of papers in front of him. "It's been five years since the first victim of the Heartbreak Killer was discovered, and police are still at a loss as to the identity of the murderer. Authorities suggest that the Heartbreak Killer is responsible for at least five deaths. Four men, and one woman. Each of the victims shares the same symbol carved into them: a heart with an X across it. While police are still—"

"Hello!" Julie shouts into the phone. "Can you hear me?"

I phase out the news anchor's voice to listen to my sister. "Sorry."

"I can hear you watching TV while you're talking to me. Do you just want to get off the phone?"

"No," I say. "I want to talk to you, I do. I just feel like you're not excited for me. Things are going well for me here, despite not having a job."

Beside the anchor is an image of a man. It's one that probably every person who lives in Windsor, or even Canada, knows. Ryan Benots. The first victim of the Heartbreak Killer. News media was plastered with his face for months after his body was found. When more bodies were discovered with the same symbol etched on their skin, media attention grew wider, beyond the Canadian border.

Suddenly, the world was interested in the murderer the media would label the Heartbreak Killer.

"I'm sorry, Emma," Julie says. Her apology actually surprises me. "I'm just—"

"Worried," I say. "I know, and I love you for it."

There's a heavy breath on the phone and for a moment I think my sister may be crying. "I was so scared when you came to us a few years ago. I know things in your life were bad. I just… want you to be safe and happy.

Promise me you'll go back to meetings if you have dark thoughts again."

"I promised you months ago, but I'll say it again. If things are bad, I'll go to a meeting." I take a deep breath. "I may not have a good job, or the best apartment, Julie, but I'm actually happy."

"I was wanting to go into the city next week," she says. "Maybe I can meet him?"

"I'm sure I can make that happen," I say. "He's been asking me about meeting you too. And worse case, if he can't see you that day, I'll bring you to the bus stop where I first met him."

As Julie laughs, the images of all five of the Heartbreak Killer's victims flash up on the television screen. My smile wanes as I look at them.

The news anchor shuffles a stack of papers on the desk in front of him. "Police don't know who the Heartbreak Killer is. Crimestoppers is offering a sixty-thousand-dollar reward for any information that leads to the killer's arrest. If you have any information, no matter how small you believe it may be, call the number below. The victims of this killer deserve justice. The friends and families of those who were brutally taken away from this world deserve justice."

CHAPTER 2

Karen

I stare at the kitchen knife in my hand, the red substance dripping onto the counter. I'm mesmerized by it. I'm completely lost in myself. The world around me is just noise.

All that's real is the knife in my hand.

"Mommy," Chloe calls out to me from the kitchen table. "I'm hungry. Where's my toast!"

My four-year-old daughter breaks my spell, and I sigh. "Honey, what's the magic word?"

"Thank you!" she says with her sweet voice, trying to make up for her previous demands.

"Not that one," I say with a smile. "The other magic word."

"Please!" She extends the word as much as possible.

I finish cutting the crust from her peanut butter and jam sandwich. I already know what will happen if I don't. A high-pitched squeal of disgust for giving her bread with crust. I know these years are precious, but sometimes a four-year-old can really drive a woman mad.

I plop her plate in front of her, and she beams. "Thank you, Mommy." She looks at the television in the living room, bopping her head to the music that Peppa Pig is singing. Soon, she starts singing along. I remind her to focus on eating. If I don't, she'll completely forget about the food she demanded I make for her.

I place the jam-stained knife in the sink and toss the crust in the garbage, which to my dismay is overfilled.

That's Owen's job to do, but I won't hassle him about it. He hates it when I do that.

Suddenly, a large hand wraps around my waist. A firm grip finds its place on my rear. "Morning," Owen says, kissing the side of my face and squeezing his hand.

I smile. I'm sure if he saw my face, I'd be flushed. Owen has a way of doing that to me. All it takes is a look from my handsome husband to throw me into overdrive. When he's happy, his face is so full of light that you can feel his happiness. It works with many facial expressions. I love it when he gives me a lustful look, one that demands I take my clothes off, and I usually do with little resistance.

But it's been a while since I've seen that face.

I turn and kiss him, and his lips make me feel weak at the knees. I almost want to tell Chloe to take her sandwich upstairs to her bedroom because Mommy and Daddy need to talk in the kitchen before he goes to work.

Owen looks at his watch and makes a clicking

sound from the corner of his mouth. "I'm going to be late. I have to get downtown for a meeting."

"Downtown?" I say, confused.

He nods. "Meeting with the owners of this old Victorian-styled house. It's gorgeous."

"That's your second one in that area."

He smiles. "That bus stop ad is really paying off. The rich folk that live there pass it all the time. That's how this old couple found me." He smirks. "They probably bought that house for less than twenty thousand. It's worth over a million now." He shakes his head. "See you tonight."

He gives me another quick kiss and leaves before I can say much more than "bye".

I watch through the kitchen window as he enters his car. As he backs out of the driveway, our eyes meet. I wave to him, but he glances away. Soon he's driving down the road, leaving me alone with our daughter… and the garbage.

I let out a sigh, taking the bag out of the small bin and tying it. When I open the front door, Chloe looks at me, her eyebrow arched.

"Where are you going, Mommy?" she asks.

I sigh again. "Going to take out the garbage. I'll be right back." She nods. I look down the road in the direction Owen left and back at my daughter. "We're going to visit Grandpa soon."

"Again?" Chloe says.

I bite my lip, hoping not to get into another toddler power struggle this morning. Why can't she just make this easy? Sometimes I want to scream and shake her, demanding she just do what I say for a change.

Chloe smiles. "Yeah! Grandpa!" She puts her sandwich on her plate. "I'm full, Mommy." She's only had three bites of the sandwich I made her. In less than an hour, she will demand more food, but that will be my dad's problem.

"Okay, Chloe," I say. "Go upstairs and get changed. We'll leave right now."

Chloe smiles, and she's about to leave the table when I remind her to wipe her sticky fingers on her napkin and to wash her hands with soap. She makes a face and audibly sighs, as if I asked her to take an epic journey across the country to the washroom when it's only a few steps away.

Instead of being triggered by it, I leave the house, closing the door behind me.

The garbage bin is already out on the corner for pick-up. Owen remembered that much today at least. I open the lid and toss the white bag on top, shoving my hand on top of it, and pushing down to ensure the garbage doesn't spill out. I wince when I feel something sticky. When I look, strawberry jam is webbed between my fingers. I frown with disgust. Seems like I too need to make an adventure to wash my hands with soap as well.

Walking back to my house, I see my neighbors in the driveway. Jason and Alice Bahers. They moved in maybe six months ago. A young couple, newlywed, less than a year married. They seem like such a beautiful pair. Both are gorgeous. I haven't spoken much to them, only the occasional polite hi and bye. Chloe has spoken more to Alice Bahers than I have. One time she was playing with a pavement chalk on the driveway, drawing a large heart and a smiley face. When I came outside to check in on her, Alice and my daughter were talking. I can vividly see the beaming smile Chloe gave Alice.

I don't know why, but I was jealous of that as well.

I've been nothing but envious of the couple since they moved in. Even now, the wife is walking her husband to his car, his lunch in her hand, dressed in a flowing sundress. She always looks her best whenever I see her. The two kiss intimately before Jason gets inside his car. They wave at each other as he drives down the road.

Her smile wanes as she notices my stare. "Morning, Karen," she says to me.

There's a brief pause before I remind myself to answer. "Hey, Alice," I say to her, feigning my own smile.

"Beautiful day," she says, fixing her sundress.

I can't help but take in how pretty she is. How young she is. How perfect she looks at this moment. I'm sure in a few months her tummy will start looking larger. I'm surprised she isn't pregnant already. The Bahers aren't bashful. In fact, I think they rather enjoy conveniently forgetting to close their drapes when they start getting intimate in the living room. Or perhaps leaving a window open. Our bedroom faces theirs.

It drives me insane, especially when I think of the

lack of noise in my own bedroom.

It feels like the entire neighborhood knows what happens behind closed doors in the Baher's home.

I realize I'm not responding to her again and smile wider. "A beautiful day," I agree. "Take care." I walk past her before she can say more and enter my house. Once inside, I close the door and take a deep breath.

Large thuds are coming from upstairs. It sounds like an elephant is stomping around. I'll never understand how such a small person can sound so huge.

I think of Alice Baher and the wonderful life she's living.

Someone should tell her the reality of what's ahead. Once a child comes, everything changes. Your marriage is forever changed. No more romantic and spontaneous nights whenever you want. No more ripping each other's clothes off when you feel like it. Now you have to wait until your little one is sleeping or when you can ensure they won't walk in on you.

No more sleep either. Even now that Chloe is four, I rarely get eight hours of consecutive sleep. She's always crawling into our bed in the middle of the night. It wouldn't be such a big deal if she laid still. She continuously moves around, kicking me as she tosses and turns, sleeping at odd angles. Somehow, Chloe could take up an entire king-size bed on her own.

Owen doesn't seem bothered, but that's because Chloe loves cuddling with me.

I think of how pretty Alice Baher looked in her

dress today. Someone should tell her how having a child changes your body as well. Nothing looks as smooth and as tight as before. Owen always admired my abdomen. He couldn't keep his hands off my midsection when we were intimate. Now he actively avoids the area because of the loose skin.

The sound of Peppa Pig singing another song breaks me from my thoughts. I hurry to the nightstand, signing off from Netflix. When I do, a news program comes on the television. The headline catches my attention immediately.

"'The Heartbreak Killer Will be Found,'" it reads at the bottom of the screen.

"We're continuing our program about the Heartbreak Killer," a newscaster at a desk says. "With me today are two of the country's leading criminologists." He looks at one of the guests. "Mr. Dadrum, before the break, you said you feel the Heartbreak Killer's identity will eventually be discovered."

The man in a tan suit nods. "That's right. I believe he will someday. Research and development in DNA will make all serial killers traceable."

The other guest, wearing a black suit, clears his throat. "I'd like to remind my colleague that there's no DNA evidence at any of the five crime scenes linked to the killer." He looks at the camera. "I'd also like to correct his statement that the Heartbreak Killer is a 'he'."

The criminologist in the tan suit shakes his head and smirks.

The newscaster nods. "That's interesting. You're

suggesting the Heartbreak Killer isn't a man?"

"That's correct," the man in the dark suit says. "We have no evidence to indicate if it's a man or woman."

The man in the tan suit shakes his head again. "Studies show, time after time, that serial killers tend to be men, specifically Caucasian men. And may I also point out that some of the victims of the killer were moved. It would be difficult for a woman to have placed the bodies in the way the Heartbreak Killer did, especially without getting caught."

The criminologist in the dark suit smiles for the camera. "That is a point many have made, however, that leads me to what I believe is the truth. The Heartbreak Killer is not one person. I feel it's a pair. A man and a woman."

The man in the tan suit laughs. "A killing couple, John, really? Impossible."

"Serial killers working together is not unheard of. The Toolbox Killers are an example."

"Those were two men," the criminologist in the tan suit says, shaking his head.

The news man interjects. "While many, even specialists in the field, continue to argue about who the killer may be, I have a question for you that I don't hear much on." He looks at the camera. "It's been five years since the last victim. What happened to the Heartbreak Killer... or Killers?" He looks at the criminologists and smirks. "And when will we see them again?"

The younger criminologist in the black suit is

about to answer when the other speaks with a booming, confident tone. "He's in prison or dead. Typically, serial killers don't stop killing. They can't control themselves. That's why the only reason *he* stopped is because he's in prison or dead."

The man in the black suit nods. "Well, for a change, we may be in agreement. The Heartbreak Killer stopped killing because something is preventing them from doing so. Death or prison are certainly reasons to explain the absence."

"Mommy!" I turn and see Chloe walking awkwardly down the stairs. "I'm ready to go to Grandpa's!"

I look at the television, where the two criminologists continue to argue. A new headline appears at the bottom of the screen. "Where is the Heartbreak Killer?"

I turn off the television, taking a deep breath. When I turn, my daughter has a wide smile and her favourite teddy bear in her hand.

"Put on your shoes, Chloe," I say. "Time to go."

She laughs. "What's the magic word, Mommy?"

I cover my face in surrender. "Please… put your shoes on."

CHAPTER 3

Owen

I'm in love. Head over heels love. The type of romance they write in love stories. The kind I never knew existed until I met Emma.

There is, of course, one problem. Karen, my wife.

As I drive down the highway heading towards the downtown area, I question what I'm doing. It's the same question I ask myself every time before I see her.

I need to see Emma every day. It's a requirement. It's like a diabetic taking their meds. If they don't take them that day, they'll feel it.

My heart will ache if I don't see her gorgeous smile. If I don't taste her perfect lips. If I don't hold her waist close to mine, the day is a waste.

I never intended to feel this way.

When I held an open house downtown, a young woman entered the house and smiled at me. I knew before she said a word she was everything I wished I could have.

"I've seen your face every day," she told me. "There's an ad on a bus stop near my home."

There was something about her smile. It was welcoming. Immediately, I shook her hand and introduced myself. She glanced at my left hand. I knew what she was looking for. A ring. I don't wear mine. When Karen was pregnant with Chloe, I gained thirty pounds. I think I was attempting to look just as pregnant as Karen did.

I got my wedding ring resized to fit my new size. Oddly, it wasn't a sense of my health or having a child that gave me a reason to lose the extra pounds. It was sales. I was a top salesperson at Windsor Realty Group. Suddenly, my sales were tougher to close.

I started a diet immediately and lost most of the extra pounds within six months. Intermittent fasting was a game changer for me. I still don't eat breakfast now. Suddenly, now that I had a distinguishable chin, people treated me differently. Sales became easier.

Once I lost the weight, my wedding ring was loose. You can't refit a wedding ring to shrink. I needed a new one and never bothered to get it.

With the look Emma gave me that day in the open house, I had never been so thankful for that decision made out of laziness.

From the moment I saw her smile, I was infatuated with Emma. It wasn't just because she was drop dead gorgeous. A ten out of ten. It wasn't just because she showed interest in me by coming into my open house just to meet the face on the bus stop bench in person. It was her whole aura.

She was pleasant. After a few minutes of talking with her, I could tell she was easy going. A person that's inviting to be around.

Essentially everything my wife wasn't.

Yes, marriage with Karen has made me bitter, but it's not just that. She was never anything like Emma. When I first met Karen, I was put off by how rigid she seemed. Before having a child, Karen was a petite woman. It would be hard for anybody not to be attracted to her, and I fell for her quickly.

I went into our relationship blind to the red flags that were shouting at me that Karen was not the person I wanted to be with. I went along for the ride anyway. Every so often, when we'd have another blow-out, I'd wonder what I was doing with her. Was she truly the woman I was meant to spend an eternity with?

In sickness and in health? Till death do us part?

Usually, the answer would be no, even when I was calm and not heated from the most recent argument in my mind. Then we'd have sex or we'd spend a fun evening together and I'd try my best not to think about my concerns.

Divorce is so messy. Was Karen such a bad wife to have to go through something so devastating as separating? Besides, every time I looked at our child, I reminded myself that it's not just me and Karen. Chloe means so much to me.

Before Chloe, I was a different man. Having a child

changed me.

A divorce would devastate my daughter. For her sake, I was willing to change my mindset and be happy with what I had in life. A marriage that I wasn't satisfied with. A life where I clocked in and clocked out. I'd coast until I was sixty-five and retired. I'd go through the rest of my life trying my best to be a good person, a good father and a good husband.

Then in walked Emma, and I couldn't stop myself.

After a few moments of talking, I asked her out for coffee. She asked when and I told her immediately.

"Don't you have to stay for the open house?" she asked, a wide smile across her face as if it's always that way.

"I need a break and good company," I told her. Her gorgeous smile somehow grew wider.

We walked a few blocks together until we hit the main strip of downtown Windsor. I spotted a coffee place across the street. It was one I'd seen a few times since setting up a contract with the listed house.

Riverside Brews. It had this rustic modern day look to it. The outside walls featured reclaimed wood with red and white bricks. An oversized floor-to-ceiling window showed the happy customers sipping on their drinks.

I'd wanted to check it out, and now I had the perfect excuse.

As we walked together, I wondered what I was doing. What mistakes awaited me with each step. It was if I knew I was walking into a different chapter in my life and willfully moved towards it.

Emma is such a wonderful talker. Every conversation brought fascinating revelations into her character. We enjoyed the same movies and had even read the same books. We talked about one of our favourite true crime books, *In Cold Blood* by Truman Capote.

I couldn't remember the last time my wife and I had a conversation without us heading towards an argument or me noticing a facial expression screaming that she was annoyed by yet another thing I'd done.

I thought of my wife as Emma and I waited at the intersection. The coffee shop was just across the street now.

An image of Karen hit me. Even in my mind, she was giving me a stare that shouted how upset she was with me. Angry at what I was doing with the pretty young woman beside me.

The "walk" sign illuminated across the street and as Emma and I started to cross, her arm swung and our fingers touched. Just the slight contact between us made butterflies explode inside me.

She pulled back her hand and smiled at me. I could almost see her blushing. It took everything inside me not to just grab her hand. I wanted to feel her skin on mine again. Instead, I smiled back, and we crossed.

The image of my wife was easily shaken as we got closer to the other side of the street.

Suddenly, another image hit me. My daughter, Chloe.

What am I doing? I asked myself. Have I forgotten that life isn't just about me any longer? I have a child. Is the woman beside me worth risking everything I have? Is she worth changing my entire life?

The butterflies inside gave a resounding answer of yes. Before I knew it, I'd crossed the street with Emma, and we were near the coffee shop.

I knew that moment that everything would change, and I would be powerless to stop it. Emma opened the door and waited for me to enter. I paused for a brief moment, taking in the sight of my beautiful date. It wasn't hard to see why I had no choice except to walk inside with her.

Emma represented everything I wanted in life. If only I'd met her before I had a child. Before I was married.

That didn't stop us though. One coffee date turned into lunch. Then dinner. Soon I was at her place. And finally, in her bedroom.

I smile as I drive towards the same coffee shop now. We make it a habit to go to it often. It's our special place.

The thought of Chloe makes my happiness wane. Thinking of my daughter as I sneak around to see my girlfriend often does. I turn on the radio to try and take my mind off things.

"Our coverage of the Heartbreak Killer continues on 108.8. We have some callers on hold who want to discuss their theories about who the infamous killer is. We—"

I immediately turn off the radio. I'm sick and tired of hearing about the killer. It's all the media in my province want to discuss. I suppose it's a slow news week if all they can talk about is the killer who got away.

Suddenly, my phone buzzes in my pocket. "Unknown" pops up on the screen.

I sigh. It's not an unknown caller. I know exactly who it is. I'd prefer it was a scammer at this point. They've called several times today already. Once while I was in bed with Karen. I quickly turned off my ringer since it was only a little after six in the morning. I texted back, pleading for them to stop bothering me. "Leave me alone!"

Yet here the number is, calling me again. They came from a different number last week. I know better than to answer any anonymous callers now.

I terminate the call without a second thought.

I turn right onto the main street downtown. The coffee shop is close. My heart beats faster, knowing that I'll get to spend more time with her. My heart aches knowing I'll see that smile. Hold her. Kiss her lips. Maybe if I truly am the salesman I think I am, we'll end up between her bedsheets soon.

The perfect start to the day. Being with the woman I love.

Love.

It's something I haven't said to her directly but feel so strongly. I've never felt the passion and love I have for Emma with any woman, including Karen. Even on our best days together, Karen couldn't give me a fraction of what Emma shows me.

Still. I'm finding it hard to continue sneaking behind my wife's back to meet with Emma. If I could wave my magic wand, Karen would just disappear. Be out of my life.

Chloe would love Emma. Emma has such a youthful presence. They'd get along quickly.

Emma is so much easier to be around than Karen. I could hear the frustration Karen had with Chloe today at breakfast. She's so miserable with everything she does.

On the other hand, Emma goes through life like it's a beautiful adventure. She floats past all the negativity.

If only Emma was my child's mother and not Karen. Life could be perfect.

Life is not meant to be perfect, though. I park my car half a block away from our coffee place and step out. A truck nearly strikes me as I do. I'm not sure if it's because I wasn't paying attention when stepping out or if the driver was in Lala Land as well.

I quickly step onto the pavement and look at the sign of the coffee shop.

Life is complicated. Karen is my child's mother, not Emma. Karen is my wife, not Emma. I made a vow on my wedding day with Karen, not Emma.

As I get closer to the coffee shop, I see Emma sitting by the large window. When she notices me coming towards her, her entire face lights up.

Instantly, mine does as well.

What am I doing? Being with Emma will only make life more complicated, and yet I open the coffee shop door and willingly sabotage everything I have for her.

She stands from her seat and holds me tightly. Our eyes meet as we greet each other. When her lips touch mine, the butterflies I had when we first met swirl inside me more aggressive than before.

Ruining the moment, my cell phone buzzes in my pocket. The light in my face dulls a moment as I know who it likely is.

As if life wasn't complicated enough, now there's Emma.

This is a mistake. Everything I've done has been a mistake.

"Are you okay?" Emma asks, her smile turning to a look of concern. She grabs my hand and stares at me intensely.

Her gorgeous blue eyes lock onto mine and all my fears go away. All that's left is Emma and me.

"I'm better now," I say, my smile naturally returning as I take in how beautiful Emma looks today.

As we kiss again, I know my life is going to get even more complicated. Being here with Emma is a mistake. One beautiful mistake.

CHAPTER 4

Emma

We order our usual drinks. In typical Owen fashion, he playfully makes fun of mine when I order. I know I'm a coffee freak. My order isn't too crazy: a venti iced half-sweet blonde vanilla latte.

Okay, I'm a coffee snob, especially when my date's order is so simple. Coffee. Black. Who asks for that? Psychopaths, that's who! And that's what I playfully call Owen as he does so.

We sit at the back, at our table near the large window. We've only been dating a handful of months, but we already have "our spot" and a designated table we always aim to sit at. I came to the coffee shop thirty minutes earlier to ensure we had it. To my dismay, it was already taken when I came.

I waited patiently at the table beside it, sipping on my first latte, waiting for the young couple to leave. As it got closer to the time when Owen and I were supposed to meet, the couple remained at the table. I was almost about to ask if they'd be okay leaving it for Owen and me, as crazy as it sounds.

I'm sure if I had, the young man and woman would've stared blankly at me in return, especially since I'd been sitting beside them for the past thirteen minutes.

Any moment, though, Owen was going to enter the coffee shop. Knowing him, he wouldn't care what table we sat at as long as he was with me. I do though.

Things are just too perfect with Owen. I feel like if I do anything that's out of order, the fantasy will end.

With all the luck I've had with men, all it would have taken is us to not sit at our table in our coffee shop for our relationship to crumble. I'm sensitive, I know. I feel like our relationship is the start of an OCD disorder. I need everything to be the same to feel as high as I do when I'm around him.

Today though, I did something out of the ordinary. I told my sister about Owen. What was I thinking? I feel like telling her how happy he makes me will curse our relationship. Somehow, me admitting that a man is making me happy will ruin it all.

That's how my life has been though. Anytime I thought I was happy, everything would blow up in my face. Then I'd start back at zero again, or worse, move back into Julie's basement.

As I sighed, thinking how frustrating my life is, I got some luck. The couple stood from my table and started to leave.

I smiled and looked at my watch. Perfect timing. Any minute Owen would be here. I discarded my half empty coffee cup. I didn't want Owen to know that I arrived early. I couldn't tell him about my table fixation. He'd think I'm crazy!

I couldn't tell him anything about how I'm feeling. I'd already made the mistake of saying out loud how happy I am to my sister. If I told Owen how much I love being with him, I knew it'd be over.

I couldn't tell him the truth. I'm head over heels for him. I love him.

How crazy is that? We've only known each other for a few months, and I feel so strongly about him. This has never happened. I'm usually more reserved. I've never been so giddy in a relationship before. I can't explain it. All I want to do is spend time with him.

I know he feels the same.

The coffee shop door opened, and I raised my head, waiting to see his face. Instead, an elderly man took his time entering. My face immediately soured until I saw the elderly woman slowly enter the coffee shop behind him. The older couple smiled at each other. The man, in a button-down white shirt, took off his fedora and held the woman's hand as they looked at the front menu near the cashier. The man whispered something to the woman, and she let out a short laugh and nodded.

I didn't know anything about this couple, but I immediately loved them. I loved the idea of them. I'd already made up an entire backstory for them. They'd been together for half a century, happy the entire time. Sure, they'd had their ups and downs, but they always had each other's back. When times were tough, they leaned on that foundation of love to get through it. They have kids and now grandkids. Both are retired, and just like Owen and I, they come to this coffee shop together because it's their spot.

Will this coffee shop be our spot forever? Will we come through the doors someday, our skin leathered, our mobility fragile, feeling just as happy as we do now?

I nearly laughed at my own thoughts. This was why I couldn't tell Owen how I truly felt about him.

The door opened, and Owen came through. He smiled wide as he approached me, holding my hands as our mouths embraced.

I felt a buzzing from his pocket and realized it was his cell phone. Suddenly, the warmth of his loving embrace let go. His face went blank. I asked him if everything was okay, and he assured me he was fine now that he's with me.

So corny.

I absolutely loved it though. I imagine he'll be one of those lame fathers who tells dad jokes all day. A future stellar parent to children.

Our children. Ugh. I'm doing it again. Stop!

One step at a time.

We sit at our table, and as always, our conversation comes easily. We somehow find the most random things to talk about and make it fun. Currently, he's telling me about his fixation with corny wallpaper in kitchens. He loves 90s-style images of bread and grapes on the walls.

For once, we're at a disagreement because I hate

the look.

Suddenly, he makes that face again. His smile wanes. I can hear the faint sound of his cell buzzing in his suit pants.

"Are you sure everything is okay?" I ask him.

His face meets mine again, and his usual charm returns to him. "Yeah, work is busy right now. Summertime is always busy. Whatever it is, it can wait." He takes another sip of his coffee.

"So," I say, taking a sip from my cup as well, "I know you said it's busy for you right now. But do you have enough time for a longer break? Maybe we can go to your place today. You can give me the official tour." I look around the room. "Maybe you can show me your bedroom first." I try my best not to look at him. If I do, I'll blush. He makes me do that so easily. Flirting with him is so hard to do without coming off shy. "Or whatever."

He smiles, and I make the mistake of looking at his handsome face. When our eyes meet, my heart melts, and my thighs warm, thinking of him between them. We haven't been in the coffee shop long, but I can't wait to leave.

He looks outside the window and back at me. "My roommate is there right now. The loser lost his job – again. He's such a scumbag, Emma. He makes everybody I bring over feel so uncomfortable. I think I've found a new place though. I may go look at it today, too."

"Do you want me to come? You know, my apartment building has a few places available," I joke.

He makes a face. "I don't know how you live where you do. I'm scared every time I walk by your neighborhood."

"And yet your face on the bus stop seems so confident." I laugh. It's a conversation he's had with me many times. The area isn't safe. He reminds me every time I see him. Yet he doesn't want me to come to his house. We've driven by his apartment though. I know where he lives, but he hasn't brought me inside.

He really hates his roommate. I was surprised to find out he had one. I assumed as a successful real estate agent he'd have a small house himself. He told me he was saving for a large downpayment. He said when he meets that special woman, he'd prefer to pick out a dream home together.

"The new place I'm looking at is in South Windsor," he says.

I make a face. "So far away from me."

"I'm sure you'll be over most nights anyway. Do you think I'd let you go back to your apartment once I have you in my house? You won't be allowed to leave the bedroom." He gives me a devilish smile, and I instantly know what he's thinking.

"So I don't suppose you're too scared to come back with me to my place right now?"

He playfully shakes his head. "Let's go." He grins as he stands up.

His wild eyes are telling me everything that's in store for me when we get back to my bedroom. I reach out for his hand, but his grin fades quickly.

He takes out his cell phone again and looks at the screen. "I really should take this." I nod as he walks past me towards the back of the coffee shop near the bathrooms. I watch him as he speaks on his cell.

I take in how gorgeous he is. He's wearing a well fitted blue suit with dark brown shoes and a matching belt. His white button up shirt fits him perfectly. He told me he manicures his hands. It's part of the business to look as good as he can, he claims.

He needs to hurry up with his phone call. I won't be able to contain myself much longer. I need him. Clothes off. Maybe I can talk him into a sick day.

He ends the call and looks back at me. I'm waiting for him to give me the same expression he had before he took it.

Instead, he gives me a thin smile as he approaches. "I have to go to the office. I'm sorry."

"Really?" If I could, I'd stomp my feet like a child being denied candy at a store. "Not even for, like, five minutes?"

"Five minutes?" Owen laughs. "We'll have plenty of time, if you can be a little patient with me. You can have me all evening."

"Well, good things are worth waiting for, I suppose," I say with a grin.

He nods. "Think about all the five-minute increments we can have together tonight."

I laugh as he grabs my waist and kisses me softly. When his lips touch mine, I don't want it to end. Owen grabs my hand and reluctantly leads me to the store entrance. This is where we say goodbye. I remind myself it's only for a handful of hours. Owen will call me when he's free.

I also remind myself that I need to slow down. Our relationship is still so new. I've never fallen so hard for a man like this, and truthfully, it's a little scary. My heart is so invested in this man that if something was to happen to our relationship, I'd be broken.

As we exit the coffee shop, he turns to me without saying a word. We both grin.

"See you soon," I say. It's supposed to be a comment but comes off more like a question. It was his promise.

Owen's different than the others I've been with. He'll be there for me. He'll be the old man in the coffee shop with his wife. He'll be like the fake doctor who's married to my sister. We will be happy. That will be us.

He leans in and kisses me. Fireworks go off inside me.

He smiles again. "I really lo—" He stops himself and looks down. "I really have to go, Emma." I can feel his cell phone vibrate in his pocket again.

"Work wants you more than me right now," I joke. "What were you going to say?" The words were on the tip of his tongue. I felt it.

He takes a deep breath. "It shouldn't take too long," he says. "When I'm free, I'll come by your place, and we can finish our date." He gives me another devilish grin and kisses me more sensually to let me know what's in store for me when he comes over.

He lets go of my waist and takes a step back. "I'll give you a ride home." He gestures for me to follow him to his car.

"That's okay," I say. "I wanted to walk back."

He makes a face. I know what he's going to say. It's not safe to walk around downtown. He doesn't know the area like I do. I'm not afraid. I've been through worse than what downtown has to offer.

"I'm fine," I say. I lean in and give him a peck. Nothing long or sensual. Something for him to think about. Always leave a man wanting more. "See you later."

I turn before he can say another word and head off. I wait for a moment and turn my head. This is the payoff I wait for. I love it when I look back and Owen's watching me leave. I love the feeling his stare gives me.

Only this time, he's not looking in my direction. He's hurrying to his car.

Something bad must be happening at work. Some fire that the company's star realtor needs to fix. I think of the face Owen had at the coffee shop. It was somewhere between frustrated and surprised.

He said he was fine though.

When I turn my head, I bump into a woman and nearly fall, but she catches me. I let out a laugh and apologize several times as I regain my footing.

"My head is in the clouds today, sorry," I apologize again.

The woman fixes her dark sunglasses on her nose. She continues to stare at me. I begin to worry that she's angry. I suppose I would be too if some random woman ran into me because they weren't paying attention.

"Sorry," I say again and walk past her. I continue down the street. I look back and see Owen's in his car, driving towards me.

He lowers his tinted driver's side window and catcalls me. His vehicle comes to a crawl. "Still thinking of you," he shouts.

I sigh. "Well, you'll have to hurry up with your work then, won't you?"

He rolls his eyes playfully and raises his window, turning his car back into the lane. I watch as he speeds off. I smile, thinking about Owen and how hard it will be to wait to see him again. I'm about to cross the street and look for any oncoming traffic.

When I turn my head, the woman with the dark glasses is looking directly at me.

CHAPTER 5
Karen

I watched as my husband kissed his secret girlfriend. I witnessed them having coffee. Watched them laugh and smile at each other from the other side of the large window. My stomach turned as they kissed again before leaving separately.

I was there the entire time. I barely concealed myself. I put on some darker clothes with sunglasses. All Owen would have had to do was turn his head and he would have seen me outside the coffee shop when he left.

Instead, he was captivated by the young woman he shared coffee with.

Emma is her name. I know that because this isn't the first time I've watched them together. It's the first time I've seen them kiss. At times, I've gotten close enough to hear them talk.

The difference this time is the emotions going through me. The pure, dark hatred I have for both of them is beyond palpable.

If I had a gun, I'd take it out as they embraced on

the street and take careful aim. I don't, of course.

Thankfully, they're parting ways. It won't be like last time, when I watched as they entered Emma's apartment building. Their hands were all over each other the entire time. I thought they weren't going to make it into her bedroom, fornicating right on the street beside her apartment door.

That time was different. I couldn't contain myself. I cried non-stop for hours. I suspected something was wrong with Owen. He started acting strangely months ago. He was so distant, awkward.

I knew something was wrong when he was happy. I knew it wasn't me making him that way. Our relationship hasn't changed. We were intimate on a monthly basis or worse. Soon he didn't bother trying to have sex at all. His sales at work were good, but nothing that would make him happier than usual.

That's when I smelt her on him. He would come home late, claiming he had late house showings and was making sales. How naive I was to believe him at first. When I asked him about the strong scent on him, he said it was one of the wives he met while closing on a house.

A few weeks later, he had the same scent on him though. How many "wives" had the same smell? Thankfully, I snapped out of my naivete. I started to track Owen.

It wasn't easy. I'd tail him with Chloe in the back when he left the house. I never discovered him doing anything wrong though. I had to come up with a new strategy.

My father, for a change, was a big help to me. He'd watch Chloe as I played detective, attempting to solve the case of who was sleeping with my husband.

I would wait for him to leave his real estate office. I knew he didn't go there as much as he used to, but he still had to keep up appearances. Besides, there's a receptionist who works at his office who I considered the prime suspect in who Owen was with.

Alexandria something. A bosomy blond-haired woman who seemed a little too friendly with Owen at the last Christmas party. I caught them speaking in private in one of the offices that night. There was something in her intoxicated eyes that told me I'd walked into a conversation they didn't want me to hear.

Emma was a total surprise.

I watch her now as she walks down the street. Owen hurries to his car. He drives right past me and lowers his window to flirt with Emma some more. I listen to their conversation in awe.

How can he not see me? I'm so close.

In her daze, she even manages to bump into me. She looks directly at me and apologizes multiple times. None of her remorseful comments are for screwing my husband though.

"My head is in the clouds today, sorry," she says to me, a wide smile on her face. I've never been in a fight in my life, but in the moment, I would have gleefully socked her right in her perfect face.

Her blue eyes look at me and she gives a thin smile

before continuing down the street.

Now what?

They're no longer together. Owen has left. What do I do with myself? Part of me wants to confront her now.

She looked right at me when she bumped into me. Unlike Owen, she saw me. She didn't recognize me.

I had wondered if this young woman knew who I was. Did Owen tell her about me? About Chloe? Did he tell her how he already has a family?

I don't even know why I bother coming back to the coffee shop again. Why do I torture myself?

I watch Emma now as she heads down the street. My feet start to move in her direction. I don't know why. It's as if my body is acting on its own. I wonder what it will do if I catch up with her. I imagine two scenes playing out in my head. One is me relentlessly beating the blond. I fantasize about un-prettying that face of hers, making her unrecognizable to Owen. Let's see if he stays with her when she's permanently ugly.

The second outcome is less satisfying but would still feel so right to do.

Tell her. I found an old image from our wedding day and saved it on my phone. When my blood isn't boiling, I imagine me showing her a picture of our wedding to see her reaction.

In my head, she shrugs and says, "Whatever, he's mine," and walks away. When she does, I viciously beat her again in my imagination.

Emma stops walking for a moment and stands near a bus stop. It angers me even more when I realize why. On the bus stop bench is a large advertisement promoting Owen's real estate services. His big stupid face is smiling at her. I cringe reading the ad copy chosen for it.

"Your dream life starts with me," it says. Owen's smile and confident posture makes it even worse. If I were a teenager, I'd buy spray paint and make the largest phallic symbol possible beside his head.

I laugh to myself at the idea but snap out of it when Emma starts to walk again. She crosses the street and walks into an alley.

I wait for her to be ahead of me before crossing. I take a moment to look into the dark alley. Despite it being daytime, the two large buildings either side block off the daylight. I make out others in the alley besides Emma. A woman clumsily rolling a shopping cart goes past her. A tall man walks like a zombie towards her. She passes him without slowing.

I make the decision not to follow her but quickly jog around the building. I don't need to go that way. I know where her destination is anyway. I just need to catch up before she gets to her building.

I wonder how such a young woman can walk past such intimidating people in the alley without a care for her well-being. The only reason I feel more confidence is because I have a weapon on me. Thankfully for Owen and Emma, it's not a gun. A large knife is sure to do damage though. I don't intend to use it today. It's just protection for now.

I'm nearly out of breath when I make it to the other side of the block. I see Emma walking across the street towards her building. Jogging, I catch up to her. I watch as she stands outside the door, sifting through her purse for her key.

I'm only steps away. For a moment, I think about the knife in my purse. What if I used it during my confrontation?

She doesn't know who I am. Emma doesn't seem intimidated walking downtown on her own. She should though. I could show her the knife. Scare her. I won't actually use it, I don't think. I just want to frighten her.

She takes out the keys from her purse and sticks one into the lock. My lips part and I have no clue what I'll do next as I get closer. Yell at her. Calmly explain to her how she's banging my husband, or plan C.

The knife.

All seem like satisfying actions.

Instead, I do nothing.

I watch as Emma walks inside and closes the door behind her. I cover my head in frustration.

What was I even going to do if I got her attention? Ever since finding out what my husband's been doing behind my back, I feel like I'm going crazy.

I have so much anger, rage, sadness. I can't decide which emotion to stick with.

At times, I'm only upset with Owen. After all, he's

the one breaking a sacred vow he made with me. He's the one doing wrong.

She's just a homewrecker.

Today, I realized that she may not even know about me. She stared at me without recognition of any kind.

But then I think of Owen and her kissing. I think of them embracing. I think of what they do behind closed doors where I can't watch them.

I walk up to the apartment door. I consider buzzing her number. There's no way to know who lives in which apartment though. Despite that, I know from previous times watching them that she lives on the ground floor.

I consider banging on her window until she peeks out her pretty little head to see me. She'll open the front door and when she does, I'll kick it open like I'm part of a SWAT team.

I wouldn't be able to arrest her, though. All I could manage is to either scream uncontrollably in her face or shout how she ruined my life.

Slut! Whore! Homewrecker!

Why did Owen do this to us? How could he do this to me?

I feel my heart is broken into little itty-bitty pieces and the stranger named Emma will take the final steps on what's left of it.

Why, Owen? Were we so bad that you had to do this to me? How did I deserve this?

I come down the apartment steps and sit on the curb.

"Excuse me," a man says, shuffling past me. It's the same one I spotted in the alley when I was following Emma. I jump at first, letting out a shriek, until I realize he's passing by me.

The dishevelled man seems surprised by my reaction as he wobbles past. In the moment, I suspect he could brandish a knife at me. I shouldn't have screamed. Maybe he had one and second-guessed using it on me. I wish he had a weapon of his own.

Finish me off. I have nothing left. Take my money. Take my life. I cover my face, not wanting to live.

How could he do this to me? Why?

And what happens after I confront him?

He'll leave me, of course. He already has his next woman waiting on the sideline. A gorgeous one at that. Younger than me. Prettier than I ever was.

I gave Owen the best years of my life. I gave him a child. I ruined my body to give him Chloe. And now he moves onto the next pretty thing that smiles at him. He moves onto an upgrade.

And what do I get?

I get to be a single mother. No doubt he'll leave Chloe and me behind as he moves on with Emma. He'll be the stereotypical divorced man who remarries younger. He'll have another family, one that he actually spends time with.

I'll be doomed to be single and spending what little time I have outside of work caring for my young child. All while Owen lives it up in his new life.

It's not fair. It's not right! I try my best but can't fight the tears streaming down my face as I sit outside my husband's girlfriend's apartment building.

"Are you okay?"

The soft voice of a woman makes me turn my head. Emma stares down at me, her light blue eyes locked on mine.

CHAPTER 6

Emma

Unsure what to do with the rest of my day, I decide to call Julie. I missed a call from her while out with Owen. She texted asking when would be a good time to visit me in the city and meet my mystery man, as she called him.

I'm about to call her when the sound of a woman shrieking startles me. I quickly stand up from the couch and look outside the window. A woman in dark clothes is sitting on the curb, covering her face. A man I recognize as one of the homeless from the area is walking near her. I've seen him around and he's completely harmless.

Still, something must be wrong. I've been tricked in the past though. In this part of town, you can never be too cautious. Lessons learnt the hard way. I sort through my purse and take out my pocketknife and slide it into my pocket.

I leave through the front door; the woman is still sitting in the same position I saw her in through my window. I cautiously walk up to her.

"Are you okay?" I ask. When she turns to me,

her face is filled with sadness. She wipes her cheek and quickly looks away. "Do you need an ambulance or something? Help of some kind?"

She sits on the curb, her back to me, and I'm regretting my decision to come outside. That's what I get for thinking I can help for a change.

"I'm…" The woman stops talking, taking a long pause. "… having a bad day." She turns to me again, sliding her dark sunglasses from the top of her hair to her nose. This time I realize I know her, sort of. The dark glasses remind me.

It's the woman I bumped into outside the coffee shop.

For a moment, I wonder if she followed me to my house but brush off the thought. Was she upset because I bumped into her? I apologized to her profusely but all she did was gawk back at me like I was a ghost.

I thought maybe she could be high. Not exactly an unlikely scenario, given this part of the city. With her being so emotional though, I can't help but wonder what her story is.

"I know you," I say. She looks up at me, her eyebrows furrowed. "I bumped into you before on the sidewalk." My paranoia can't help itself from thinking the most extreme. This strange woman followed me to my house. "Is that why you're having a bad day?" I ask.

She pauses a moment and shakes her head. "No." She clears her throat. "My mother passed away years ago. We used to live in this area. I guess I wanted to walk around a bit and reminisce."

I let out another breath, feeling terrible for asking her such a question. No wonder she looked so out of it when I bumped into her.

My mother's been dead for over a decade. I think of her every day, especially around Mother's Day, holidays or special moments.

I almost want to tell the woman about our shared similarity but hold my tongue. I don't want to be that person who ups someone's bad day, especially when they're so emotional.

My mother was taken from me. Hers likely died of cancer or an accident of some kind. My mother's death was no accident.

Suddenly, I want to sit on the curb and start bawling with her.

"I'm so sorry to hear about your mother," I say.

She stares at me through her dark-rimmed sunglasses. Despite how dark they are, I can see the outline of her eyes.

"Thanks," she says.

I'm not exactly a people person. I'm more of a stay inside and watch Netflix kind of gal. I'm not sure if it's because this stranger tugged my heartstrings with our shared motherly loss or if it's because she's so emotional, but I can't help myself.

"Well, I live in this apartment," I say, nodding behind me. "If you want, you can come and have some tea or something. Coffee?"

She gawks at me again and I immediately regret asking. I know the answer is no. Why would a crying stranger want to come inside another stranger's home?

I don't even know why I asked to begin with.

"That's okay," I say, answering as if the answer is no. "You seemed like someone who could use someone to talk to, and, well, I could use good company. I'm sort of new in the city."

She gives a thin smile. "That's nice of you. Maybe another time."

I smile back. "I'm Emma." I lower my hand to her.

Instead of shaking it, or saying anything, she looks away and slowly stands up from the curb, dusting some dirt off her leggings. She puts her hand inside her purse and moves it around inside.

"I'm Karen," she says, still rummaging inside her purse. She looks at me for a moment and takes a deep breath. "I appreciate you checking on me, but I have to go." She pulls out her hand and puts it to her side.

Without saying another word, she turns and leaves down the block. I can't help but watch the woman named Karen walk away. I can hear her muttering something under her breath as she shakes her head to herself.

CHAPTER 7

Karen

I can't believe that just happened. The entire time I walked back to my car, I continued to think about my interaction with my husband's mistress.

I can't get over it. When I get home, I'll write about it in my journal. Owen bought me a nice leatherbound one last year for my birthday. It even has my name on it. Despite the gesture, I tend to just complain about him in it. And now about his perfect mistress.

Emma. Ugh.

She's so nice. A strange woman is crying outside her house in a rough part of town and she comes out to check up on me?

When I watched her from far away, it was easy to tell she was a beautiful woman. Up close, it's different. I got a sense of what kind of a human she is immediately.

Kind. Caring. Compassionate. Beautiful. Gorgeous.

Essentially everything I'm not. I can't help but compare myself to her, especially since we're sharing the same man.

I've been sitting inside my car, replaying everything in my head. I think of Owen and my hand turns into a fist. I slam it onto my steering wheel, causing the pathetic horn on my Honda Civic to blurt out a squeal.

No wonder why he picked her over me. What chance do I have to keep my husband when she's my competition?

When she started talking to me on the curb, I immediately wanted to spill everything to her. The more I was in her presence though, the more I hated her.

I nearly made a scene. In my mind, I ran through the different scenarios, from me screaming, "you stole my husband," to somehow crying even more and in between sobbing tell her the truth.

One thing's for certain. She doesn't know about me. I suspect, given how wholesome her aura was, that she likely doesn't know Owen is married either.

How much of the truth did Owen tell her? Does she think he is separated? Divorced? Does she know about Chloe?

I need to know.

If I were a stronger person, I would have accepted her invitation for tea. I could have learned so much about who my husband is screwing.

An image of them being intimate hits me. I can imagine them kissing. Him caressing her tight body. I feel nauseous thinking of it.

I almost wish it weren't her who Owen chose. Why couldn't it have been that receptionist from his office instead? She was much less pretty, older. She had a nasty attitude to boot. I believe the phrase is resting bitch face.

No, instead Owen had to sleep with Emma. I go over our interaction again, her trying to console a stranger on the street whose mother passed away.

That is not entirely untrue. Mom died over five years ago from breast cancer. I feel terrible using her in my lie, but it was the first thing to pop into my head. Mom lived nowhere near Emma's area.

I consider going back to Emma's apartment and knocking on her door. I could show her the picture of Owen and I. Reveal the truth.

A terrible thought hits me. What if she finds a way to forgive Owen? What if they stay together? I cannot bear the thought.

Owen will move on with the perfect woman, while I am alone. He'll move on, happier than ever, while I'm broken forever.

I try my best to shake the thoughts I have. I have never felt so low in my life. I see the Ambassador Bridge in the distance and imagine running my car off it into the fast-moving water below.

Then Owen would get everything he ever wanted. One less wife, one new girlfriend. A whole new life.

I clench my fist again, but with my hand still hurting from my last assault on my steering wheel, calmly open my hand. "Just give me a sign," I say to myself. "Please. I do not know what to do anymore. I do not know how I can fix my life. Give me a sign."

I wait a few moments and look around outside. Of course, no actual sign pops up. I wish it magically could. Something that would tell me what to do. As I drive away, the only thing I see is Owen's bus stop bench ad, mocking me as I leave.

CHAPTER 8

Owen

Just when life is perfect, my past sneaks up on me. The calls continue. It used to be once a day, not several. Calls. Texts. No matter what I say or do, they won't stop.

It threatens everything I have. I feel like an anvil is hanging over my head and at any moment, it could fall.

I think of Emma and my heart sinks. I've never felt this good ever. Emma makes me feel like the man I always wanted to be. But it could all slip away if I don't do something.

With the phone calls increasing, I know I'm heading towards an end that won't be good. That's an understatement. A nuclear bomb will go off in my world if I don't handle this right.

I take a deep breath, driving down the highway. It's not fair. I shake my head and bang my fist on the steering wheel. I tighten my face and can't hide the rage inside me.

It's not fair that this is happening to me now.

I'm not heading to work. That was a lie. After I

spoke on the phone, it was clear that I couldn't stay there. I had to leave, or else things would get worse.

The last thing I want is to drag Emma into the mess I've made. Thinking about what Karen will do if she finds out about Emma is enough to drive me insane, but what if she finds out everything I've done?

I'm ready to move on from Karen. My past coming to light would make a divorce much trickier. I'd get pummeled in court.

I suppose I'm more worried about Emma. What will happen if she discovers I'm not the man she thinks I am?

Why did I have to lie to begin with? I could have told her any number of lies that made more sense. Instead, I went with a nasty roommate. I guess Karen counts as that.

I should have said I was separated. I should have mentioned I had a daughter. In the moment, I couldn't. I just wanted an opportunity to talk to Emma. Get to know her. I couldn't be upfront. If I had, she might have lost interest.

As if my life couldn't get worse, my cell phone vibrates in my pocket. When I slip it out and look at the screen, it says it's from the anonymous caller again. I shout and strike the steering wheel.

I can't ignore this. I answer the phone again. "Yes!" I shout. "What is it now?"

"That's no way to talk to me, Owen."

My blood is boiling already. I can't help myself.

"Just leave me alone. I'm done with this. You need to stop calling me. Leave me alone!"

I terminate the call immediately before they have a moment to respond.

My phone vibrates with another call as soon as I lower my cell. I feel my hand shaking with rage.

I shouldn't, but I answer the phone again. "Leave me alone, I said!" I'm about to shout every four-letter word I can think of when I hear her sweet voice.

"What's wrong?" Emma asks. "Why are you mad at me?"

I take a deep breath and slow down on the highway. My head is spinning. "Sorry, Emma. I thought you were someone from work."

"What's going on, Owen?" Emma asks. I can hear the confusion in her voice. "You were acting really weird with the phone calls at the coffee shop, and now you're shouting on the phone. You can tell me. I called to check in on you because you seemed so out of it. I was concerned. Now I've upgraded too deeply worried."

I take another deep breath. A car behind me honks several times. I realize I'm in the fast lane, going twenty under the speed limit. "Hold on," I tell her, lowering my cell. I pull over to the side of the road, putting my hazard lights on.

I cover my face, trying to keep it together. When I feel ready, I pick up the cell. "Hey," I say in a soft voice, hoping to reassure her that everything is fine, despite it being anything but.

"I'm worried," she says again, not letting me off the hook. "What's going on?"

"Nothing," I answer but obviously she's not falling for this lie. "Okay, I'm having some issues at work with a coworker. It's getting a little heated. He's calling me, threatening to go to management. It's a long story and not worth getting into. Believe me. It's going to be okay. It will be sorted out soon. We're bringing in management and we'll talk this out. I'm okay." There's a long pause. "I'll be fine. Don't worry. I just hate tension at the workplace. I typically avoid drama."

"Okay," she says. "I just want you to know I'm here if you want to talk."

I laugh. "Well, you're the perfect girlfriend, so I know you are. Thanks for calling," I say. Moments ago, I was so full of rage, but just speaking to Emma for a few minutes has talked me off the edge. "You really know how to make me feel better."

She laughs again. "I didn't do anything."

"You sure did," I say. "You're just you. Perfect."

She sighs. "Well, I guess that means you need to get to know me better. I'm far from it."

"You'll have to tell me more about that when I come over."

She laughs again. "I hope you deal with this work issue soon. I can tell it's stressing you out. I also hope you hurry up and come over!"

I smile. "As soon as humanly possible, I'll be at

your door, I promise. See you soon."

"See you soon," she says back.

"Love you." The words slip out of my mouth innocently. I didn't mean to say them. It's all I wanted to say to her, but have kept it inside, worried that my emotions are moving too fast.

She doesn't say it back though. Instead, I hear nothing. The call ended.

Did she even hear me? Part of me wishes she didn't. I don't want the first time I said I love you to be an accident while getting off the phone.

My phone vibrates once. A text. It's Emma. She must have heard me. I look at the screen, and my smile vanishes instantly.

It's not Emma.

I look at the words, the rage returning to me quickly.

"There's no going back after what we did together."

CHAPTER 9

Karen

The three of us sit at our dinner table. Chloe shovels her vegetables from one side of her plate to the other, picking at the asparagus every so often. Why is it that eating is such a struggle for her? I know parents can't stand fighting with their children about eating, but she's underweight, according to the doctor. I've already reminded her several times today to try and finish her food.

Owen is doing the same. Picking at his meal. I nearly demanded he eat his food as well the last time I said something to Chloe.

Only I know the reason Owen isn't eating. It's not hard to guess. He has other plans tonight.

He's still dressed in his suit. Typically, when a day is over, he'd change into comfy clothes for the evening. Even when he has houses listed and at times will need to leave suddenly to meet potential buyers, he'd wear his baggy clothes around the house.

Comfort above all else. Not tonight, though.

Is he having dinner with his girlfriend tonight? Will they go straight to the bedroom instead? Watching them, I could feel their chemistry. It's palpable.

I hate it. Owen and I never had such chemistry. Having now talked to Emma herself, I can see why he's so infatuated with her.

Chloe pushes a piece of broccoli on her plate with her fork, and it falls onto the table.

"Chloe!" I say, losing my cool. "Eat it! Don't play with it."

Chloe makes a face of resistance. "Mom. I hate broccoli! You know that."

"Just eat it!" I shout. Chloe looks at me, surprised, and so does Owen.

I cover my face, trying to fight back the tears. How can I sit here and pretend to not know what my husband is up to? Why does it come so easy for him to break my heart continuously? What did I do to deserve this?

He's a monster.

"Do what Mom says, pumpkin," Owen says to Chloe.

"Dad!" Chloe says with her toddler tone that can drive me mad.

"Eat three pieces of broccoli and you're off the hook," he says.

"One!" she shouts back.

Owen laughs. "I'm not negotiating with a four-year-old." I can feel his glare on me. I uncover my face and see his concerned look. If only he could read minds, he would know it's because of him.

"How was your day?" he asks.

"Fine," I say, feeling a tear welling in my eye. I quickly use a napkin to cover my face and wipe it.

"I went to Grandpa's," Chloe says, matter-of-factly. "He played dolls with me."

"He did!" Owen says with a playful voice. "Grandpa's funny."

Chloe laughs. "Yes, he is. We had a doll party, and he put on music."

A single laugh escapes my lips. Chloe and Owen both look at me for a moment, but when I continue eating, the two continue their conversation about the doll party at Grandpa's house.

My father truly is a changed man. He had more than an average temper. He never hit me, and as far as I can tell, he wouldn't strike Mom either. But every other type of abuse was at his disposal, and he wasn't afraid to use it.

He would call me every terrible name in the book. Mom as well. I don't know how she put up with it. He'd break items around the house when his temper reached its boiling point. A few times, he made multiple holes in our walls. A few days later, he'd fix them, as if it never happened.

I never forgot though.

Now he's playing dolls with Chloe and having a party with them.

It's so odd to me. I wish he treated me a fraction as well as he treats my daughter. I wonder if I would have turned out a better person if he had.

After my mom passed, Dad was broken.

The cynic in me thought he wouldn't know how to take care of himself and would rely on me to do that for him. That wasn't the case, though. I thought he'd be even more angry being a widow, but that wasn't the case either.

I had to ask him once, what changed? I was in awe and a little jealous of his change in temper. I know I have his rage, his anger. How could he make such a turnaround in life?

Anger management was the answer.

I was shocked when he told me. It took my mother dying for him to realize he needed help. He also told me that me having Chloe helps him remember why he doesn't go back to his old self. He loves being a grandpa. My mom never got to experience that.

Five years ago, she died. My dad went from being a monster to the type of father figure I always wished he could be.

Owen clears his throat and wipes his mouth with a napkin. "I really should get going," he says. "I lined up a few visits with the listing downtown." He looks at his watch and smiles at me. "This is their second visit. Fingers crossed for a sale. The wife really wants it, but the husband is reluctant because of how old it is."

"Really," I say coldly. I'm in awe of my husband now. How does lying come so easily? I know that none of that is true. "Fingers crossed," I repeat with a thin smile.

Owen stands up from the table, bringing his dish to the kitchen. He comes back and wraps his arms around my shoulders, kissing me on the cheek. "See you later tonight."

It takes all of my emotional control not to break down and cry. His lips are soft when they touch my skin, and I imagine the same mouth kissing his mistress tonight.

"Night, broccoli head," Owen says, messing his hands through Chloe's long hair.

"Dad!" Chloe shouts. "Look, I ate three broccolis. Am I done now?"

Owen's about to answer when I interrupt. "Eat!" I demand. "Everything on your plate. Now!"

Owen looks at me, confused. Chloe resists and looks at her dad. I slam my hand on the table, causing her to jump. "Eat what I said!"

Chloe's large eyes meet mine, and I can tell what she's wondering. "What's wrong with Mommy?"

A lot is wrong with her. If only you knew what I've been thinking. If only you knew what I want to do tonight.

Owen looks at me and back at Chloe. "Do as your mom says." He turns to me, a look of concern still present on his face.

"I hope you close the deal," I say, a thin smile on my face. I wish he could read my mind right now. It's full of murderous rage and it's all directed at him.

I watch as he leaves. Chloe is humming some song as she slowly eats off her plate. She stops when she sees me looking at her.

"Mommy, why are you crying?" she asks innocently.

I didn't even realize tears were coming down my face. I quickly wipe them. "I'm fine."

"Did you poke your eye?" Chloe asks. "I did that, and it made me cry."

I let out a laugh. "No... hurry up and finish your food. We're going back to Grandpa's."

"Yay!"

I give in to Chloe and she doesn't finish her plate. I swear children can tell when you don't want to deal with them.

I don't know why, but I'm going to do it again to myself. I need to see them together. I'm not sure what I'm hoping for. Maybe a part of me hopes to witness Owen coming to his senses. Breaking things off with her and staying with me. Realizing the importance of not just me, but our family.

That's the real fantasy. It won't happen. Emma is the improved version of a wife he wants. He knows it. I know it.

As I get changed into my dark sweater and leggings, I think about what I want to do tonight. I have a plan. A mischievous one. Ever since I thought of it, I can't help but smile.

Before we leave, I sit at my desk in my home office. I wish I never agreed when Owen said I should take a year off to spend more time with Chloe. I thought it was a great idea at first. I enjoyed my work from home job, but thought I could use a break. Now, all I do is sit in my misery all day while my husband screws women behind my back.

I open my desk drawer and take out my journal, reading some of the earlier entries. These were the ones I wrote when I was happy. When Owen was truly mine. Usually, it was just poetry that I was inspired to write. As I turn the pages, my words become sadder and darker. No more poetry, only four-letter words and a lot of exclamation marks.

After I found out about Emma, my journal entries were nothing like the ones I started with. I read some of the later entries to motivate myself to go through with my plan.

I hurry Chloe into the van and think what I'm going to do. If I'm not careful, I could easily be caught.

Wouldn't that be something? I'd have a lot of explaining to do.

I worry if I really want to do this. As I get closer to my father's house, I second-guess everything. Maybe I should turn tonight into a visit with dad.

Another surprising thing for me to say. When I was a teenager, I dreamt of ways of escaping my house and being free from my father. I couldn't wait to be living outside of his reach.

Now that he's had his "aha" moment, I actually enjoy his company. I never understood how my mother could have fallen for a man like my dad. With his temper always on edge, I couldn't imagine him being romantic with my mom, or charming, or anything but frustrating to be around.

But I have to admit, I'm enjoying his company more and more. Sometimes we play old card games together like cribbage or old maid while Chloe plays with her toys that my dad bought her.

I used to think I'd never be like my father. I'd never have his temper. I imagined I'd be more like my mother with Chloe. Lately, though, I've been on the edge, just like Dad was with me.

I hate what I'm becoming and yet I can't stop. I know it's going to get worse, especially if I go through with what I intend to do.

As we pull into his driveway, Dad opens the front door, and Chloe shouts, "Grandpa," inside the van. A wide grin appears on his face.

"I didn't expect you two tonight!" he says. "Chloe, do you want some ice cream?"

"Dad," I say, shaking my head. "You always hop her up with sweets."

"Well, that's because she's so sweet," he says. He

turns to his grandchild and kneels. "So, chocolate or vanilla?"

She smiles. "Chocolate!"

"I knew it," he says with a smile of his own, the wrinkles on his face showing his age. With his expression, you would never have suspected he was a terrible parent. He's the stereotypical happy grandpa now.

"With sprinkles!" Chloe adds.

"Of course!" My dad laughs, turning to me. "And what does my daughter want? Chocolate or vanilla?" His smile is welcoming. Part of me knows I should go inside his house, have a scoop or two with him and Chloe. Watch *The Price is Right* or whatever program he's watching tonight. Beat him in cribbage.

"I was hoping to run a few errands, Dad."

He nods and looks at Chloe. "Go inside, kiddo. Take out the ice cream from the freezer and the sprinkles from the pantry. You know the drill." Chloe laughs as she heads inside.

Happy that Chloe is off my hands, I'm walking back to my van, wondering where to start with my plan.

Am I really going to do this? Out in the open? It wouldn't take much for me to get caught. The police would be called. My life would be over.

I think of Owen and Emma, embracing. The whole world around them is just noise when they're together.

"Karen." I turn and my father is following me

down the driveway. He walks up to me, concerned etched in his wrinkles. "I have to ask, is everything okay at home?"

For a moment, I think of telling him everything. Part of me hopes if I do, I'll see the old him come back. I could use the angry version of my dad tonight. I'm surprised he even asked me.

"Just busy right now," I tell him.

"You know I love having Chloe over," he says, clearing his throat. "You know that. I love having you over too, but it's been a lot lately and usually without you. Are you burnt out or something? I know from past experience that having children isn't easy."

I can't lie. I'm not made that way. It doesn't come as easy for me as it does with Owen. But instead of answering him, I go to the van and open the door. "It'll only be for a few hours, Dad. Is that okay?"

He pauses a moment and folds his arms. I've seen this look many times before, especially when I was younger. Usually, it would be followed by shouting and swear words. But instead of the evil face he'd have when he stood this way before, he's full of worry.

"Of course," he says. "Enjoy your time."

I'm thankful that he's not harassing me for answers. I'm thankful for many things my dad does for me these days. Especially when I need to use him to dig deeper into what Owen is doing behind my back.

As I step into my van and turn on the ignition, Dad walks into his house, and I put my mind to how to carry out what I want to do.

    I will enjoy my time tonight.

CHAPTER 10

Emma

My entire body is satisfied.

Owen turns to me in bed and smiles. I know he's thinking the same thing. That's something I can't get over, how in tune we are with each other.

Having sex with Owen is so synchronized. Our bodies just know what to do with each other to give maximum pleasure. We bring the best out of each other in the bedsheets.

He knows exactly where to kiss me to get the desired outcome we both want. We lay in bed with each other, completely naked, our bodies sweaty from the cardio workout we just finished.

And this wasn't our first round of exercise tonight.

When he first got to my apartment, I couldn't help myself. I needed him. I wanted him in me right away. It's all I thought about since we left the coffee shop. It was like he was my drug, and I needed to take him in order to think straight.

After that, we managed to eat dinner together. I'm not a good cook. That's something I was very open about from the beginning. If he had any fantasies that I was some dream woman who cooks, cleans and does the dishes, he had another thing coming.

I'm more of an order delivery kind of girl. Paper plates when I'm feeling super lazy.

After some glasses of wine and slices of pizza, we were energized for the second round tonight. From the look Owen is giving me now, I can tell we're not done either.

I wrap my leg around his and kiss him again. As I do, I can tell he's getting more excited. I attempt to slide my body on top of his, but he playfully pushes me off.

"I can't." He laughs. "I need to breathe, Emma."

"Oh, come on, old man."

He makes a face. "Seven years older than you. You make it sound like I'm robbing the cradle." He sighs. "Now, where are my pants?"

I shake my head. "No need for those," I say with a thin smile. "We're just having a cool-off period and then back to work."

"Oh, is that what we're doing?" He smiles. "Well, sorry to ruin the mood, but I need to pee."

He kisses me before standing up from the bed. I take in the view of his lean body as he stretches in front of me. I'm waiting for him to leave, but he stares at me instead.

"What?" I ask nervously. I see his eyes on my bare skin and can't help but feel the need to drag him back into the bed. I shyly grab a sheet and wrap it around me.

"When we talked on the phone before, you didn't hear what I said to you, did you?" he asks.

"What do you mean?"

He smiles. "I was worried that you heard me. I didn't want to say it to you like that."

I laugh, not understanding. "What are you talking about? You said something to me before I got off the phone with you?"

He nods. "Good. I'd rather you didn't hear it that way."

My eyes light up. "Well, you can tell me now if you want?" I say, unable to hide the schoolgirl smile on my face.

He climbs back into the bedsheets, his body on top of mine, as he kisses me softly. I can feel him stiffen between my legs as our kiss continues and his tongue enters my mouth.

"First, I have to pee," he says with a laugh.

I smack his shoulder. "So romantic."

He laughs as he stands back up. "You don't know the half of it." I watch as he leaves my room buck-naked, his unusually small rear swaying with each step.

It's something I find so cute about him. Owen is very handsome, lean and slightly muscular. With his frame, it was surprising when I discovered he was lacking in the ass.

I can't get over how quickly my life turned around since meeting him. After the last incident with my last job, I was close to just moving back to the country and back to my sister's basement. I had attempted to be a waitress again, but my boss was a little too nasty with his demands and tone. I quit on the spot.

After another failed job, I was beginning to feel cursed. No matter what I did, I'd have bad luck staying in the city.

Then Owen strolled into my heart, and my whole life changed for the better. I've never felt a man give me so much attention the way he has. I feel his love just thinking of him.

Now, as I wait for him to return to the bedroom, I know my life will change again. Once he says those three words to me, things will escalate even quicker.

I love you.

I can visualize him saying it. I feel it. I want to say the same to him. Thinking about how happy I am at this moment makes me teary-eyed.

I never thought I'd find love like this. I never saw what love looked like. I'm sure my parents loved each other at some point. I hate the idea that Julie was conceived from a night of drinking and bad decisions, followed by me soon after.

As far back as I can remember, though, my parents did not love each other. Well, that's not entirely true. My mom was head over heels for my dad. She would have done anything for him. I'm not sure why she felt so strongly about him. He was a drunk. An abuser.

A cheater.

I'm not sure how many women he slept with behind my mother's back, but I know of one. Mom took us, Julie and I, when we were children, in a taxi and stalked Dad around the city. I remember how shocked I was when I saw Dad kissing some random woman on the street.

When I looked at Mom, she was beyond shocked. She just looked broken. I half expected her to get out of the taxi and scream and yell at Dad and the young woman. Instead, she asked the driver to take her home.

The whole way back, she had the same expressionless face. Julie tried to get Mom to talk. She was confused.

"Mom, why was Daddy kissing that woman?"

Despite being a year older than me, my sister was a little dense at that age. It was obvious even to a child like me.

When we got home, she locked herself in her bedroom and wouldn't answer the door when Julie knocked.

"Mommy, what's wrong?"

Eventually, I got Julie to leave her alone, telling her she was upset about Daddy.

"Why?" Julie asked, so innocently.

I didn't know how to explain it at that age. I

don't even remember what I said. But I got Julie to come with me to the living room and watch television. It's wonderful how you can easily escape what's happening around you by watching a cartoon at that age. The world could be erupting around you, but if you can watch *Power Rangers* while it's happening, it's not so bad.

That was until Dad came home. Mom opened the bedroom door when he did. She had the same expressionless face she had in the taxi, only this time, a large kitchen knife was gripped in her hand. She lunged towards Dad, cutting him deeply in the arm.

Julie screamed. I stood up from the couch. I wanted to help, but didn't know who to assist.

Mom managed to stab him in the chest before Dad overpowered her. I was frozen, unable to move except watch in terror as my parents tried to kill each other.

I remember vividly my mom shouting continuously, "I hate you! I hate you!" Dad shouted back, trying to get her to calm herself.

Julie would tell me later that it was her who called the police. When they arrived, they arrested both my parents.

An officer drove us to our grandparents on our mother's side.

No matter how many times we tried to get information about what was happening with Mom and Dad, our grandparents wouldn't tell us. We stayed with them for months before we knew what was happening.

Mom was in jail and wouldn't be coming back

anytime soon. Dad left. He never returned.

It breaks my heart thinking about it. What happened when Julie and I were children impacted the rest of my life. Sometimes, I wonder how Julie can be so well put together and not crazy. She lived through the same trauma as I did, yet she managed to have a functional life. Married to a doctor, sorry – chiropractor, have a child, live in a beautiful house.

Meanwhile, I had nothing. Nothing, until Owen.

He loves me. I know it, and once he says it, I too can have everything Julie has. I deserve it too.

I deserve to be happy.

A vibrating sound on the nightstand breaks my thoughts. His cell phone screen lights up.

It's his work again, more than likely. He told me about the problems he's been having. Suddenly, it vibrates again, then again.

I think of the coffee shop and the face he made when his phone vibrated. I'm not a snoop. I trust Owen. At least that's what I tell myself, even as I reach for his cell phone.

I feel sick to my stomach as I read the messages on the screen.

"You and I aren't through! I need to see you again!"

CHAPTER 11

Karen

Dressed in black, I wait outside Emma's apartment, every so often peeking inside to see what they're doing. Only I can't now.

They've been in the bedroom for the past hour. A *whole* hour!

I can't remember the last time Owen embraced me for longer than a few seconds. Meanwhile, he's inside having a marathon with pretty little Emma.

The thought of it is driving me insane. I don't know why I continue with this. Why am I letting this man ruin everything in my life?

I could easily call him out. Instead, I'd rather let everything get to such extremes first.

I have a plan tonight, and every so often when I think about talking myself out of it, I look in the window and remember where my husband is. He's not at our house. He's not with our child. It's not us in that bedroom.

He's with another woman. A better woman than

me.

I put my head up and peek through the ground floor window, staring into Emma's living room. The light is still on. The half-eaten pizza and sodas are still on the table.

Owen and Emma aren't there though. Even when Owen and I were at our peak together in our relationship, our intimate encounters would only last minutes.

I hear a rumbling near me. I turn and see a disheveled man wheeling a shopping cart. I recognize him as the same person who frightened me earlier today. He stops when he notices me. It's obvious what I'm doing. I'm right beside the window, peering in. This man has caught me.

Our eyes meet. He arches his eyebrow before continuing down the road.

I let out a breath and take my hand out of my purse. I hadn't realized my fingers were searching for the kitchen knife I brought with me. I told myself that this was a rough area, and I needed it for protection, although part of me thinks that's not altogether the truth.

I've thought about using it. Every time I've stared into Emma's apartment and saw that bedroom door closed, I thought about breaking in and using the knife on both of them.

Even in my dark fantasies, I get overpowered by one or both of them. In my imagination the police come and arrest me and take me away.

I slide down the side of the apartment building,

covering my face. What am I doing?

I truly have lost my mind. Maybe I should call the police on myself. Or drive to the nearest hospital and admit myself for being psychotic.

Breaking into her apartment wasn't my plan tonight. Compared to what my mind's coming up with, my goal tonight is much more childish but feels oh so right.

I stand up, taking one more glance into the apartment, fueling myself to go through with what I wanted to do. When the door remains closed, I have the motivation to go through with it.

I quickly make my way to my car that's parked a few blocks over. When I get inside, I only have to drive a few more blocks before I'm where I want to be.

"Your dream life starts with me."

I read the bus stop bench ad with my husband's face on it and my expression sours. Is this what I have? A dream life?

I've been living in hell since I found out what he's been doing behind my back.

Nobody sees Owen the way I do. They only see what he wants them to. The handsome, lean, well-dressed realtor who can sell your house quickly. The top salesperson at Windsor Realtor Group. I look at Owen's handsome face, his perfect smile staring back, mocking me.

It's time people see Owen for what he really is.

I reach into my purse and take out what I bought from the store after dropping off Chloe at my dad's. I shake the spray paint can several times before I start desecrating my husband's ad.

I've never attempted graffiti before, but I must say, it's not bad work. It's not hard to paint a penis. I make sure the one I spray beside his face is huge. As big as the lies he's been telling me.

I smile as I even take the time to draw a large vein going up the side. I stand back and laugh, taking in the view of the mushroom tip facing Owen's face. I think next time I could improve on my depiction of testicles though.

It's childish, I know, but this is what I came up with to feel better, and it's working.

Owen is a dick. Everyone needs to see it for themselves.

CHAPTER 12

Owen

I splash water on my face, smiling at myself in the mirror. It doesn't get better than this.

I'm excited and nervous to go back to the bedroom. I know she'll be waiting for me. I know what I'll tell her. It's the words that've been on the tip of my tongue the past week.

I feel giddy inside just thinking about how this will go. I'm in my early thirties and yet feel like a high school boy who's fallen in love for the first time. After seeing what I have with Emma, I wonder if I ever actually experienced love before her.

I could have said it to her before leaving the bedroom, but I want to prolong the moment, plus I enjoy messing with her. I don't want the happiness inside me to end. I wish I could feel this way every day.

I could.

The only thing standing in my way is Karen. If only I could make a wish and have her disappear, my life would be perfect.

If it wasn't for Karen, though, I'd never have Chloe.

The thought of my daughter is ruining the special moment I'm about to have. Why does life have to be so complicated? Why didn't I meet someone like Emma to begin with? Why did I marry a woman like Karen?

Her temper is beyond what I would consider normal. Trivial things can send her over the edge. She hates it when I don't do chores to her liking, typically redoing what I've cleaned. In the morning, she's typically moody and anything but welcoming or positive.

We've talked about her anger issues at times. She blames her father for her temperament. Meanwhile, her dad's a sweetheart. She tells me he was different when her mom was alive. I wasn't in the picture at that time though, so I never witnessed how her father used to be.

I splash more water on my face, trying to get thoughts of my wife and child out of my mind. I can't have them there when I go back to the bedroom. Back to Emma.

I need to be present with her. There's no going back once I tell her I love her.

Things will only get more complicated, and yet I don't care anymore. I just want to be happy.

I stare at myself in the mirror, my smile beaming back at me. I know I'm a lucky man. Some people never experience the type of love I have with Emma.

When I open the bedroom door, my smile wanes when Emma's putting on her clothes. She doesn't look at me as she wiggles herself into her tight jeans.

"I should get some sleep tonight," she says. She finally manages to look at me. "I need to put out some resumes tomorrow, and I want to get an early start."

My mouth drops. This wasn't how I expected this to go. "Are you struggling with money? I can help you."

"No, that's okay," she says firmly.

I'm about to close the door behind me but my hand slips on the loose doorknob. "Maybe I can help you tomorrow. We can grab some lunch after. Maybe we can even take a look at that apartment I told you about." I fiddle with the loose doorknob. "This place doesn't suit you."

She stares at me blankly but doesn't say a word. She walks past me, her lips tight. When she comes back into the bedroom, she has a rusted toolbox in her hand. She places it on the bed, opening it. After a moment, she finds a screwdriver and walks up to me.

She kneels near me and tightens the doorknob, tossing the screwdriver back into the toolbox.

"This place suits me fine," she says.

I can't help but smile, but her stoic face has me worried. "What's wrong?"

"Nothing," she says. "I just need to go to bed soon."

I look at the doorknob and the toolbox. "I'm impressed. A handy woman. You even have your own tools."

She lowers her head. "It was my father's toolbox."

It hits me. She hasn't told me much about her mom

and dad, but I know both are not involved in her life. What I do know about her dad is that he left her a long time ago.

"You don't talk much about your parents," I say. "You know, you can share with me." I smile. "I want to know everything about you, even the sad things." I give her a thin smile.

For a moment, our eyes meet, and she looks down. "The toolbox is all I have from him." I wait for her to share more, but she turns her head to the toolbox. "I think you should go. We can see each other tomorrow."

This is not going at all how I thought it would. We were supposed to be smiling, laughing, making love, anything but this.

"Did I do something wrong?" I ask.

She shakes her head. "I know what you want to say to me, and I'm not sure I'm ready."

I take a step back. How could I read her so wrong? I thought she was head over heels for me. I suppose I was wrong.

"I see." I reach for the doorknob, again impressed how quickly she fixed it. I'm not sure I even know how to do such small maintenance tasks around the house.

"Wait," she says. When I turn to her, a tear is going down her face. "It's not easy for me, falling in love. I've had my heart broken so many times. I want us to be different. I just need to know that you won't hurt me."

I take a step towards her. "I would never, Emma." Before I can say another word, she stretches out her arm and hands me my phone.

"You forgot your cell," she says. I take it from her as she wipes her tears. "Sometimes when you say what you want out loud, it ruins everything. That's always been my problem. Goodnight, Owen."

I take the hint and leave the room. Whatever is happening with Emma, I'm sure she'll explain at some point. What is apparent is that I'm not wanted here.

It's only when I'm outside of her apartment that I look at my cell phone and read the unread messages. My confusion turns to anger as I reread each word.

Emma must have seen them. For a moment, I consider knocking on the door and explaining everything, but I know that's a terrible idea.

I read the messages again and shake my head. Everything is falling apart. My house of cards is starting to wobble. I know what will happen next.

I won't let it though.

CHAPTER 13

Karen

It's a new day, but there's nothing new about it. It's the same as the day before and the day before that. Another day where I feel my sanity is slowly breaking and I'm becoming someone unrecognizable.

There was a time where I thought I was a terrible human being. Years of therapy helped, but what really made a difference was meeting Owen.

There was a time where I felt he was my entire world. I loved being around him, spending time with him. Making love to him.

Now he's someone else's world. All the things I used to love doing with him, he's doing with another woman.

Last night, when he came back much later than I expected, he snuck into our bedroom and into our sheets without saying a word to me.

He knew I was awake. He looked right at me but didn't say a word.

What did I expect him to say though? "Hey Karen, I just came back from sleeping with my girlfriend and realized what a terrible husband I've been. It's over with her. I know you're the only thing that matters in my life."

Now that's truly something that would only happen in my dream life, and of course that world starts with Owen.

I feel stupid after what I did to his bus stop ad. How childish can I be? I'm in my thirties. This isn't exactly the time I thought I'd start my graffiti crime career. Still, the amount of joy it brought me in the moment was unlike anything I've ever experienced.

Besides Owen making up with me, I've had other fantasies, much darker ones. When he came back and climbed into our shared bed without saying a word, I imagined taking the pillow he fell sound asleep on and stuffing it in his face.

He'd obviously overpower me. In my fantasies, I can't win either.

What if I grabbed a knife from the kitchen while he slept? The idea kept me rolling in bed for hours. I could finish our nightmare marriage with a few well-deserved slashes.

At one point, I even slipped a leg out of bed as my impulses began to get a hold of me. The only thing stopping me was realizing that I'd have to sneak past Chloe's room to get to the kitchen.

The idea of that stayed with me. Instead of going through with my dark fantasies, I continued to let them play through my mind, enjoying them only in my thoughts.

When Owen's alarm went off in the morning, I realized I hadn't slept much at all. All I could do was think about how my life came to where it is now and how much I wish I could end it all.

I just want the pain to stop.

After waking up, it was just like any other day. Get Chloe changed, fed and let her watch cartoons. Ensure I cut off the crust from her bread, otherwise I'd hear her little shouted demands of me. Another day of cleaning the house. Waiting for my husband to come home after a long day of work and having sex with his floozy girlfriend. Enjoy whatever scraps of attention he's able to share with me and start over the next day.

I sit at the kitchen table, every so often reminding Chloe to keep eating her peanut butter and jam sandwich I made her that she's been pecking at for more than ten minutes. I threaten to turn off the television if she doesn't eat, but if I do that, she'll just annoy me until I agree to put it back on.

Being a parent isn't easy work. Being a parent in the middle of a mental breakdown is even harder, almost impossible.

I look outside the kitchen window and spot the garbage bins still by the curb. I forgot to bring them in last night. Again, our house is the only one on the block not to have their bins off the street. I can only wonder what they think of us.

I hurry outside, throwing on a light jacket, and

grab the bin, dragging it up the driveway.

"Morning, Karen," my neighbor Jason says to me with his usual warmth. His gorgeous wife, Alice, is following behind him to the car to wish him goodbye.

"Hey, Jason," I manage. "Good morning, Alice."

I stop dragging the bin when she kisses her husband on the lips before he gets into his car. She watches him leave as I remind myself not to stare at them.

When I bring the bin beside the house, I'm nearly in tears. How can this be where I ended up in life? I never thought what Owen and I had together could go down such a dark path.

I never thought I'd be this upset. This rageful. At any given moment, I'm either in the process of crying or exploding with anger.

When I saw the neighbors embrace, I wanted to roll them over with my garbage bin, breaking their perfect moment together.

When I go inside the house, Owen is there.

I hate myself even more for not being able to find the courage to talk to him. Tell him the truth. Tell him I know everything he's been up to. Tell him how much I hate him. Explain that I just want his love. Why is that so hard to give?

I worry if I do tell him what I know, I won't be able to contain my anger. The dark fantasies I have could become real if he makes up more lies and twists the truth.

I want to shout in his face, "Why? Why do this to

me? You loved me, didn't you? Did you ever? If you did, how could you do this to me?"

"Good morning," Owen says to me. For a change, his usual greeting isn't warm or fake. He seems just as deep in thought as I am.

"Morning," I say, unable to agree that anything about today is "good".

Instead of grabbing my rear or kissing my cheek before running out the door, he stares at me. For a moment, I actually wonder if overnight my hopes have become a reality. Will Owen change today? Will today be the day he realizes how much he has in our marriage? Will he tell me the truth?

"It'll be another late night," he says, shattering the dreams I have. "Sorry, I know I've been absent a lot lately. Work's been frustrating. Should get better soon, I promise."

I turn my back to him and start cleaning the remaining dishes in the sink, including Chloe's dish on the counter with a half-eaten sandwich. She giggles as she watches her cartoon on the couch.

"That's fine," I say.

I wait for him to smack my rear as he usually does. Instead, he gathers his things and begins to leave. I never thought I'd crave even the small gestures of attention he gives, but I do.

Am I such a terrible wife that even a small kiss on the cheek and a smack on the ass is too much to ask? Does Emma now get all of his attention, with not even crumbs left for me?

I don't say bye to him. I won't say a word. Instead, just like any other day, I'll drop off Chloe at my father's house and continue my spiral into madness.

Before he leaves, his phone rings and he answers it. "Hey," he says. I realize it can't be Emma he's talking to. Or does he even care at this point and is willing to speak to his girlfriend on the phone with me in the room? "I'll be at the office soon," he says quickly, calming my anxiety about who he's talking to.

I wash Chloe's plate and put it on the drying rack.

"What?" Owen says with a surprised tone. "Really? Graffiti?"

I smile as I wash the coffee mug he used this morning. It's his favourite. One that Chloe picked out with me for his last birthday. A black mug that reads "One Proud Papa". Suddenly my day is turning around. I actually get to hear Owen find out about my dirty deed. I cover my mouth with my hand, water dripping on my shirt. I can barely contain my laughter.

He sighs. "What do you mean? ... Oh, well that's good."

Good? What does he mean? How can what I did to his bench ad be good?

Owen laughs as he hangs up. He walks up behind me, chuckling to himself. "You'll never guess what happened."

I try to contain myself before turning to him. One smirk from me and in my head, he'll somehow piece it together. It was me who did it. When I feel ready, I turn to him.

"What was that about?" I ask, putting on my best Oscar performance.

"Some kids spraypainted a penis beside my face on that bus stop ad I have downtown." He laughs again.

This wasn't the reaction I was hoping for. Shouldn't he be upset? Slightly aggravated? Worried what others will think when they see the ad?

"They didn't use permanent spray paint," he says with a smile. "Overnight, there was a bit of rain and it washed some of it away. The office is sending someone over to clean the rest of it off." He shakes his head. "Stupid punks."

Stupid punks? More like a dumb thirty something woman who can't even commit misdemeanors properly.

I bite my lip to stop myself from screaming. "How stupid," I agree. I didn't read the label properly. I just chose the glossy black paint.

His smile wanes as he meets my eyes. For a moment, I wonder if he can see how much I hate him as he looks back. "Well, I should go. Busy day. See you later."

I watch as he leaves. No kisses. No hug.

I think of our neighbors. I imagine them kissing goodbye. I see how happy they are together. I imagine how happy Owen will be when he embraces his dear Emma again later today.

I take Owen's favourite mug from the drying rack

and smash it on the ground. Pieces of ceramic fling across the floor. The word "Papa" remains intact in front of my feet.

"Mommy!" Chloe shouts as she jumps off the couch and looks into the kitchen. "Oh no. Watch your feet."

I try my best to compose myself as I look at my innocent daughter. "Get ready to go to Grandpa's." She looks at me wide-eyed and I relax. My tone was rougher than I hoped.

For a change, Chloe manages to get ready to leave and is in the van quicker than most days. I'm thankful. I look in the rearview mirror and notice Chloe doesn't have her seatbelt on.

"Seatbelts on!" I shout.

"Okay, Mommy," Chloe says with a slight tone. It aggravates me but I don't take the bait. She takes forever to put her belt on.

When I turn on the ignition, the radio starts, cutting into a familiar broadcast.

"The identity of the Heartbreak Killer remains a mystery," the AM broadcaster says. "With it being five years from their last reported murder, the city of Windsor has just one question: Will we ever see the return of the Heartbreak Killer? The serial killer who used duct tape to bind their victims and carve their infamous symbol in their victims is now legendary in the city. We—"

My mind drifts as I listen to the broadcaster. A small smile breaks on my face as evil thoughts intrusively strike me. What a wonderful fantasy. What a brilliant idea.

The city wonders when the Heartbreak Killer will return, if ever. Perhaps I can help.

"Mommy," Chloe says in the backseat, breaking my dark thoughts. "What's a serial killer?"

I turn and smile at her. "Ask your dad that question." I turn off the AM station and put on some classic rock. The idea of how to solve everything hits me again.

"Change of plans, Chloe," I say, putting the van in reverse. "Instead of going to Grandpa's, we're going to the store."

CHAPTER 14

Owen

"Where are we meeting?" As soon as I'm alone in my car, I text to confirm.

Within seconds, I get a reply. "Our usual place."

I take my cell phone and toss it on the passenger seat. Part of me wants to lower my window and whip it outside. That's one way to end the antagonising calls and texts.

Only I know better. If I do that, it will get worse. Much worse.

This doesn't end well. The stakes are about as high as possible. My entire life could be ripped apart if the truth comes out, and I know if I don't do something, it will.

I can't ignore it any longer. If I stop answering my phone or text messages, I know it will only go from bad to a complete nightmare.

It's not fair.

Finally, I have something I feel is worth living for

and it could all go down the drain.

I think of Emma, and I know instantly she's worth the fight. I need to give this my all. After last night, Emma may suspect something's up.

After all, how many lies can I tell her before the truth slips through? This wasn't what I wanted. If I could, I'd go back and tell her the truth.

I'm married. I'm not happy. I plan on leaving her. I worry what the truth will bring to our relationship. I can't imagine not seeing Chloe every day. My daughter makes a huge difference in my life. Before Emma came along, spending time with my daughter was all that kept me going.

It's not Chloe's fault that I can't stand her mother. It's not my daughter's fault that I don't love her mom any longer.

But Chloe will be used against me. I already know that if the truth comes out, Karen will be in full scorched earth mode. I know her temperament, and it's not easy to deal with. She won't stop until she breaks me.

Then again, she's not the only person in my life with those intentions.

I didn't ask for this. None of it. I just want to be happy. I want to be happily married. Have many more children. Live a life full of love and laughter, where I feel special.

Karen doesn't do that for me. Emma does.

I think of the phallic symbol that some kids spraypainted on my bus stop ad. At first, I laughed it off, thinking it was some dumb teenager with no life and a hatred for the structured world.

What if it's not?

What if it's all related? What if it's them?

I was told to meet at our usual spot. The Tim Hortons in East Windsor, close to my office. When I get there, I'll be sure to bring up the graffiti.

I stew in my thoughts as I get closer. My frustrations break when I see the coffee shop ahead. It's still early, and only a few cars are parked outside in the lot. Most are in the drive-through, the cars trying to get their last-minute brews before hurrying to work.

It takes only a moment for me to see her. She's leaning against her white truck. She brushes her curly blond hair over her shoulder as her eyes lock onto my car. She smiles immediately.

I never asked for any of this.

Emma came into my life unexpectedly at an open house. My life was forever changed the minute we spoke to each other.

Before her, though, there was Alexandria Sutton. Her smile widens as I pull into the parking lot.

Unlike with Emma, the moment Alexandria came into my life, my life was tarnished forever. I can't help but notice how gorgeous she looks this morning. She's wearing a tight red blouse that leaves little to the imagination. I don't need to think too hard about what's underneath since I've already seen it.

She waves at me, and I lower my head, opening the car door. I remind myself of what I need to do. Her calls and texts need to stop. I need to reason with her.

There's only one problem. Alexandria is certifiably psychotic.

CHAPTER 15

Karen

When we park at Home Hardware, the small home improvement store near our house, Chloe groans. "Mommy, this store is boring!"

I sigh. "Just need to grab a few things, Chloe. Be a good girl and afterwards we can get some ice cream."

"Yay!" Chloe shouts enthusiastically.

That should give me enough time to get through the store with her, I think. When we enter, Chloe scurries up to a cart, but I shake my head. "I just need a few things. I don't even need a cart."

"But, Mommy, my feet hurt!" she claims.

I shake my head. Doing anything with a child takes ten times longer. And how is it possible that her feet can hurt? She's been sitting in the van for the past fifteen minutes as we drove here. Before that, she sat at the kitchen table and on the couch watching television. Yet, somehow, she claims her feet hurt as if she's been on them all day.

I know better than to get into a power struggle with my four-year-old. I grab the cart and pick her up, placing her gently inside. She smiles as I push her through the aisles looking for what I need.

I find the first item quickly.

"Hold this," I say to Chloe, handing her a roll.

"What is this?" she asks.

"It's called duct tape," I answer.

"What does it do?" she asks with another question. I know that after I answer this one, another one will pop in her head.

"To tape things together," I say with a thin smile.

"Why do you need duct tape?"

I sigh. "To tape things, honey. No more questions."

All I need is one more item, and yet I can't find it for the life of me. The store is massive. It could take me forever at this rate, and my partner in crime is getting annoying.

"I want ice cream, Mommy," Chloe demands. "Chocolate ice cream." She licks her lips and smiles.

I know she's just being a kid, but it's aggravating me to no end. I'm regretting not bringing her to my dad's for a short visit. I thought I could get through this without many issues. I wanted to give my dad a break from watching Chloe. I may need him to watch her a lot more soon enough.

Still, to figure out how to proceed properly, I'll need

a lot of time to think. Think without constant pestering. Even if I turn on her favorite cartoons, she'll continue to bother me with demands.

"Mommy, I'm hungry."

"Mommy, can I watch YouTube?"

"Mommy, I need to pee."

Of course that means I'll have to accompany her to the bathroom. I know I'm supposed to cherish these moments with my daughter at this tender age. She won't remain four forever. Still, I wish she was a little more independent, especially right now.

"Mommy's almost done," I reassure her.

An employee walking past me nods and I ask him where I can find box cutters. The man directs me to go down aisle three and to look on the right side halfway down.

I looked down that aisle already but make my way there again. I'm halfway across the store when my thoughts wander.

I've been obsessed with the coverage of the Heartbreak Killer. I enjoy listening to most true crime stories but especially about this serial killer. The HBK, as some call the murderer, was known to bound their victims with duct tape. After the victim was killed, it's believed HBK used a box cutter to carve the symbol of a heart on their skin, with an X going through it.

The symbol is what made the Heartbreak Killer infamous. HBK only murdered a few people, but it was the way they did it that cemented their reputation.

Sometimes, they'd even humiliate the victims by taking off their pants or moving their bodies to embarrass them even in death.

As the employee said, I find several box cutters in aisle three. I can't help but be thrifty and pick up the cheapest one. I slide the button on the box cutter, revealing its blade, and place it against my skin to feel its sharpness.

"Mommy, don't hurt yourself," Chloe says, wide-eyed. "It's sharp."

I laugh. "It is. Mommy will hold this one. Don't lose the duct tape though."

Chloe nods. "Now can we get ice cream?"

I smile and nod with her. "Vanilla, right?" I say playfully.

"Mommy!" Chloe laughs. "Chocolate."

Chloe tells me about a cartoon she wants to watch when we get home. My hope is that with enough sugar and television I can work out my plan.

I roll up to the cashier, a young man with spiky blond tips. He smiles at Chloe as she hands him the duct tape.

"Thank you," he says with a childish tone.

"You're welcome." My daughter smiles. I'm pleasantly surprised by how polite she's being.

As he rings it through, my mouth drops when I hear the radio behind him. It appears I'm not the only one who enjoys listening to coverage about the Heartbreak

Killer. The radio host talks about the serial killer and reads off a number that people can call if they have any information that could lead to the murderer's arrest or capture.

"Is that everything?" the cashier asks.

I hand him the box cutter. He looks at me strangely as he rings it through.

The radio host continues to read off the number to call for information about the Heartbreak Killer as the cashier tells me the total. I wait for the teenager to realize I'm buying the exact items used in the Heartbreak Killer's five murders.

I smile awkwardly when I realize the kid couldn't care less. After I pay, he wishes me a good rest of my day.

It will be.

First, ice cream. Second, planning a murder.

CHAPTER 16

Emma

When I first met Owen, my whole life turned around. I thought he was too good to be true. Turns out, maybe I was right.

I try not to think about it, but it hasn't left my mind. I'm not the type of girl who looks at her boyfriend's phone, but I did with Owen. I saw those messages. I can't unsee what I read.

He told me things at work haven't been going well. That may be what it is. I think of the message over and over again.

"You and I aren't through! I need to see you again!"

That's ambiguous enough that it could be a coworker wanting to reach out to figure out a resolution to the problems they have with Owen.

Or it could be another woman.

Stupid. How stupid am I? Instead of addressing it, I passively kicked him out of my apartment.

I thought I was braver than that.

I never understood why my mother didn't confront my dad with his infidelity. Instead, she chose to go after him with a knife. I didn't think I was like that. I never thought a man could have this effect on me.

I thought Owen was the perfect man. If I'm wrong about that, what else could I be wrong about? What if there is another woman in his life?

What if it's me who's the other woman? Of course, a handsome man like Owen must have been swooped up already. I can't imagine how a man of quality like him could be single. He'd have to be a secret psychopath not to be married with children at his age with what he has going on in life.

All day I've been like this. For the past few hours, all I've been able to do is sit on the couch and watch news and documentaries. Most are centered on the Heartbreak Killer. I used to find these kinds of shows interesting. Now it's just background noise as I figure out what to do.

This morning, I went for a run. I'm not exactly religious, but I do believe in signs. I asked for one to help me figure out what to do with Owen. I asked for a sign. During my run, I ran past his bus stop bench ad. It was on purpose even if I couldn't admit it. I needed to see his face.

But talk about a sign. I saw a young man with a bucket and washcloth cleaning the bench ad. There was some black smudge covering half his face that the man was cleaning.

I have to admit that I didn't expect such a clear sign. It was plain as day. I thought Owen may not be telling me the truth. He's hiding something from me. He's not the man I think he is. When I came across his face in the ad, someone was cleaning it. What I thought was dirty is being cleaned.

I almost laughed out loud as I ran by the ad. "Your dream life starts with me," Owen promises on his ad. Maybe he still can.

Before what happened with my mom finding out about my father, she was the hopeless romantic type. One time we watched an old Disney movie and Julie asked when she would find her Prince Charming. Mom said the perfect man was out there for each of us, we just had to be open enough to find him. When we did, we shouldn't give up on him. I still remember her face when she told us, "Never give up on love."

Seeing what happened with her and Dad sort of changed my perspective on that memory now, but she had a point.

Owen could be my person. The one I've been searching for. My Prince Charming.

I shouldn't shut myself down. I can't close my heart to how I'm feeling.

I also shouldn't be blind.

My mom was too blind to see what my father was doing and look at what that bought her. Look where that brought Julie and me. Years of trauma. Therapy. A terrible dating life. A terrible, terrible dating life. It's worth repeating.

I know I need to be brave. I don't need to confront Owen aggressively or anything like how my mom handled the situation. I can come at him with questions.

Who was that who texted you these messages? Are we exclusive?

It's a question we haven't talked about. Maybe there is another woman, and it's because we never established boundaries. We've been together for months though. The other day he was about to say he loved me. It's hard to imagine there could be someone else, especially when I can feel how much he cares for me.

Perhaps he's a good actor. He is a salesperson after all. Has he talked me into buying his lies?

I think of Julie and her husband, David, the *doctor*. It would be easier to go back to the county and live with her. David offered me a part-time job as a receptionist at his office. He doesn't have enough patients to require two receptionists. I know he was only offering it to help me. Yet I refused. I wanted to make it on my own in the city.

I'm not sure what I'm trying to prove.

I imagine how ironic it would be for me to work at my brother-in-law's chiropractor's office as a receptionist, answering the phone with, "This is Dr. Bersmene's office. How may I help you?" Meanwhile mocking his doctor status every chance I get outside of work.

Our banter would somehow lose its charm if that was the case.

I audibly sigh. I think about ordering a pizza but realize I still have leftovers from last night. The pizza I shared with Owen.

I sigh again.

All I want is a good man. Why is that so hard for me? With my past, I was likely doomed from the start.

Unable to understand what's happening in my life, I do something that surprises even me. I call my sister for advice.

Thankfully, she picks up right away. "Hey," she says cheerfully.

"Hey," I say back with a less than enthusiastic voice.

With my unusual tone and cadence, Julie's concerned right away. "What's wrong?"

I don't tell her right away. I'm having a hard time finding the words. "Do you ever think of her?" I ask instead.

Right away, she knows who I'm talking about. "Sometimes, yeah. It's hard not to now that I'm a mom myself."

I take a deep breath. "That makes sense. I've been thinking about Mom a lot lately. Dad too."

She sighs. "Ugh. Don't get me started. I mean, our dad is useless. Mom though. It's sad for me to think about."

I can imagine how my sister feels. We both suffered through the trauma of not having our parents in our lives. After our grandparents who raised us both passed away, I truly felt like I had no one left except her.

Owen changed that to two people, or so I thought.

"Why are you thinking of Mom?" Julie asks. When

I don't say a word, I can hear her take a deep breath. "You need to let go of the past, Emma."

"More therapy?" I joke. "I didn't find it as helpful as you did."

"You never took it seriously," she says. "You still carry around Dad's old toolbox. It's like you're holding onto the past. It's, like, symbolic."

"What?" I say, confused.

"It's like you think you can fix what happened to us, Emma," she says softly. "You can't, though. You need to let it go. Just toss out that toolbox."

I scoff. "I don't want to talk about Dad anymore, okay? I didn't call to talk about him."

"So, what's wrong?"

"It's the mystery man," I say in a mocking tone.

"Really? Why? I thought things were going so well. What happened?"

A part of me already feels stupid for thinking my sister was the shoulder to cry on. I think of her making fun of me for what I'm about to share. Putting me down for how I could be so foolish.

"I'm worried there's another woman."

"What!" Julie says, shocked. I'm surprised by how she's taking this. She doesn't even know Owen's name and yet she's stunned. "I mean, you mentioned him to me, and that's something you rarely do, so I thought it was going really well."

"I did too. The other night I read one of his

messages on his phone. I know. I shouldn't have, but he's been out of it lately. The message was from an unknown number, and it said, 'You and I aren't through! I need to see you again!'"

"Really," Julie says. I thought she would immediately tell me I was right to suspect something was up, but instead she asks more questions. "Why do you think there's another woman? Besides the text message?"

I sigh. "Well, for one thing, I haven't been to his place. It's been months that we've been seeing each other and I've never been to his apartment."

"Come on, Emma," she says with an irritated voice.

"What?"

"Why hasn't he brought you to his place?"

I take a deep breath. "He told me about this situation with his roommate. He's in the process of finding a new place."

I wait for Julie to dig into me some more. Tell me how stupid I am to have had the blinders on for so long. I think I called her for that purpose, to kick me when I'm down.

"I'm sorry you're going through this, Emma," she says instead.

I feel a tear welling in my eye and quickly wipe it away. "I just wish I knew what was happening."

"Why can't you ask him?" she says. "You need to have a long conversation about your concerns. Hard questions. You deserve answers."

I sigh again. "I know. I'm worried he'll leave."

"If he does, he doesn't deserve you."

I let her words sink in. I want him to be what I thought. He makes me happy. He makes me feel special, like I'm the only one in the world.

"Either that or you can follow him," Julie says.

I know she's joking, but I'm not in the mood. "I just want to be happy. Why is that so hard?"

"Emma," Julie says softly. I wait for her to dig into me about moving back with her and David. Stop making life hard on myself. Go back to therapy. Ask if I'm drinking again. Talk to me about rehab or starting AA meetings. A tear is running down my cheek. A sign of my emotions. I used to think I was made of stone. Nobody could hurt me. Here I am, about to shatter like glass.

"I love you," Julie says finally. "I just want you to be happy. No matter what's happening, just know that I'm here. You don't have to go through it alone this time, okay?"

I smile, wiping away my tears. "We always did have each other's backs, didn't we?"

"I'm here for you, Emma," Julie reminds me. "Whatever you need." She takes another deep breath. "I can go to a meeting with you again if you want. Like how I did last time, when you needed someone to go with you the first time."

"I can do that on my own, Julie, but thanks."

I hear the faint sound of Rowan in the background.

"Is that Auntie?"

I laugh. "Put him on. I need to be cheered up."

"Okay," Julie says. "I love you. Just going to say it again. Here's Rowan."

"Love you too," I say. A moment later, my nephew's cheerful voice greets me.

"Auntie!" he says. "How are you?"

"Good," I lie. Despite that not being the truth, talking to my nephew even for a moment has managed to cheer me up instantly. "How's the Gravedigger truck?"

"Good," he says, not getting into much more detail. "Are you coming over soon for a visit?"

I take a moment, thinking of Owen. "I think soon, buddy. Maybe even a sleepover at your place." I smile as he asks if we can play when I come to his house.

CHAPTER 17

Owen

Alexandria flashes me her devilish smile. It's one that she's brandished around me many times. It's what made me fall for her to begin with. She could give me a look that said she wanted to strip my clothes off and screw without saying a word.

It's what caused our innocent exchanges at work to turn into a full-blown affair. Most of the realtors talked about what a smoke show Alexandria was. One of the new guys, some kid named James, said he managed to kiss her after work at a bar. Nobody believed him. She was way out of his league. Whether he was telling the truth or not, he struck out when he tried to sleep with her.

I later told her the truth about what was happening in the office behind her back. Ever since she started at Windsor Realtors Group, some of the guys had a running bet on who would nail her first. I, of course, was not in that group, being married, but it would come up at team lunches. All the men took their shots, sometimes multiple ones, and each got denied instantly.

But there was something about our exchanges

that I thought was different from the others'. Maybe it's because I was married and wasn't afraid to talk to her. I didn't feel the need to bloat my ego around her or flirt.

I could be myself. I'd make light conversation with her at the office when I arrived. I'd stroll by her desk to talk. One time she bought me a coffee. It was an innocent gesture, at least I thought so at the time. She had bought one for other coworkers too.

I bought her coffee too. At one point, it turned into us going out for coffee during work time. The guys at work joked about how she was my work wife, one time even saying it to our faces as we talked at her desk.

I laughed it off, but she just smiled at me. The same one she's giving me now as I approach her.

If I could go back in time to the Christmas party, I'd never have kissed her. I don't know what I was thinking. Karen was at the party. Despite my wife's presence, I couldn't help myself. Alexandria was looking gorgeous with her tight Christmas sweater that had little bells where her nipples would be.

When we found ourselves having a private moment in one of the offices, the conversation became awkward. The tension grew. Our bodies got closer to each other. Next thing I knew, we were all over each other.

Karen interrupted us. If she hadn't, I wonder how far things would have gone had I been smarter and locked the door.

After that, we saw each other often, but not as friends. It was a full-blown affair. I didn't love Alexandria though. Our relationship was nothing like what I have with Emma.

I just wanted Alexandria. Her body was like a drug. She oozed sexuality, and I just wanted to have her body. I craved it.

When I finally got smart and broke things off, Alexandria wouldn't back down at first. She called the landline in our house once too. I don't know what would have happened if Karen picked up the call. Alexandria and I had a very candid conversation though, and after that, she stopped.

Suddenly, she's back in my life again with a vengeance. Texting and calling me. Harassing me. The idea of her infuriates me. I don't care how good of a lay she was, I told her it was over. Why can't she get it through her thick skull that I'm not interested?

Now, as she looks at me the same way she did when we were alone at the Christmas party, her gaze has no effect on me. In fact, it makes me sick. All I want to do is shake her and get her to stop.

"Why do you keep calling and texting me?" I say, getting straight to the point. "I thought we talked about this."

"I know what we had was special," she says, putting her hands up, pleading with me as I look away. "I can't stop thinking about us. I know how we ended things wasn't the way we wanted it to go. I know we can have something special again."

I shake my head. "I'm not interested. You know this."

"I've tried dating. I don't feel the same way with them as I did with you. I know you felt the same."

"It was only for a few months, Alexandria. Now, you have to stop."

She glances down, taking a moment before looking at me again. "You told me you loved me. Did you mean that? Because I love you, Owen. I love you!"

I look around. Even though nobody else is in the parking lot except the cars driving by, some have their windows down. "Let's just keep it down, okay?" I plead.

"Did you love me?" she continues. "Did you mean a word of it?"

I lower my head. "I was confused. I'm married, Alexandria. I have a child. I can't do this with you. You need to stop calling me."

She lets out a laugh. "Being married doesn't stop you, Owen… It's not fair what you did with me. What we shared was special. I know it, even if you won't admit it."

"I'm married!" I shout again. A driver creeps past me, taking a sip of his coffee that he got from the drive-through. I look at Alexandria, who's now fully crying.

Great.

I wonder if she thinks this will make me feel anything for her. It doesn't. All I am is pissed off. She needs to stop harassing me.

"I'll tell your wife everything!" Alexandria shouts.

She turns away from me and I grab her arm, gripping her body tightly so she can't wiggle away. "You will not say a word. Do you hear me?"

"I'll tell her everything you did to me. Everything we did. I'll tell your daughter what kind of man her daddy is!"

With her mention of Chloe, my body acts on its own in a fit of rage. My arm moves from her hand, up her chest towards her neck, holding it tightly for a moment. Alexandria's eyes widen in fright as she attempts to smack my arm away. I grip tighter.

A moment later and her face turns red. Her sultry eyes become fearful for her life. A car starts to drive past us, and I immediately let go of her, taking a step back, smiling as the car passes. When it's out of sight, I look around as Alexandria starts to cough uncontrollably. Her hands cover her neck, and she looks up at me in fear.

Shocked at my own actions, I'm even more worried by what I say next to her. "You say a word to my wife, or you come close to my daughter, and I'll kill you."

CHAPTER 18

Karen

I've been thinking non-stop since the answer to my problems hit me like a sack of bricks. It's been hard to be a mother to my child with such terrible ideas swirling inside me. I put on cartoons for Chloe as I sat in the office, the door locked, my mind at work. I even used my journal to jot down my initial thoughts.

I know I'm losing it, but I'm not sure I was ever really sane to begin with. My journal is a testament to that.

I had to put aside my project once I realized what time it was. It's nearly seven at night and although it's still daylight outside, I wanted to start the night routine early with Chloe to get back to my thoughts. Back to my plans. Things will connect easier with a sleeping child.

If I treat this like I did the bus stop bench, everything will go wrong.

I step out of the office and ask Chloe what she wants for a snack. She refuses, saying she's not hungry. I know, though, that if she doesn't eat, she won't sleep.

How am I supposed to go through with what I want to do if I can't even get a four-year-old to eat a snack before bed?

We agree that tonight it will be cut up carrots and cucumbers with ranch sauce to dip into. As I cut the vegetables, I know my effort is fruitless; no matter how much I make, she'll eat a few of each and tell me she's full. Then an hour later, after her bath, when it's time for bed, she'll demand more food.

I won't fight her at all tonight. I'll go with the flow in the hopes of getting her to bed as soon as I can. I need to be meticulous with my planning. There's no room for error or impulse.

Most of my plans I've already run through in my mind. I just have to write them out to ensure there's no room for error.

The front door opens, and I'm surprised to see Owen step in. He gives me a thin smile as he puts his briefcase on the bench by the door. He takes off his suit jacket, rolling up his blue button-up shirt before approaching me.

"Hey," he says.

"Daddy!" Chloe shouts, running up to him, hugging his leg. Ranch sauce from her lips stains the bottom half of his shirt. Usually he'd be annoyed, but instead he runs his hands through her hair and kisses her forehead.

"I wanted to come back early," he says. "To see you guys. It's been a rough day at work."

I can see on his face that he means it.

Something happened today. Did Emma and him break up? Something else? Maybe this is just a work issue, but I've never seen him look this exhausted. Even when a sale falls through, he seems to have a natural positivity, believing another is around the corner. Tonight, his eyes are puffy with dark circles and his expression blank.

"I can't stay for long," he says. "I have a night showing soon. I just wanted to stop by for a bit."

My heart sinks. So much for a breakup. I know exactly where he'll be going. How stupid can he think I am? How many late-night drinks with coworkers or evening showings can he possibly have?

Owen looks down at Chloe. "How about we give Mom a break with bath and bedtime and Daddy do it?" Chloe smiles and nods. Owen lets out a laugh and runs his hand through her hair, messing it again. "Follow me, little lady."

As he passes me, he smiles. "I know you've been doing a lot, so I just wanted to come by and help before getting more work out of the way. Things will slow down soon."

I purse my lips and put on the best performance I can manage. "Thanks." I'm not a good performer.

He walks past me towards the bathroom with Chloe following close behind. I hear him put on the bath water and my daughter and husband talking. He laughs at something Chloe says as she giggles. While this beautiful moment plays out, all I can do is think.

He didn't come for me. He doesn't care about me. After he's done spending quality time with his daughter, he'll leave and be unfaithful again. He'll break his vows once more.

In a few months, it will be our five-year anniversary. Before I found out about Emma, I asked him what he wanted to do for our special day.

"It's only five years," he said.

"Half a decade," I responded. "That's worth doing something." I put out the idea of going back to the same resort we stayed at for our honeymoon in Cancun. He said he'd look into it but wasn't sure if he could take the time off.

I'm sure that wasn't the case. He was probably already falling for pretty little Emma.

I walk into the bathroom and Chloe is splashing Owen with water from the tub as Owen makes a playful angry face.

"That's it, little girl!" he shouts. "You're going down!" He turns on the tap from the sink and splashes it on her. Chloe shrieks and giggles more.

I take in the moment, questioning my impulses, but instead let the words escape my lips. "I'm going out for a little," I say.

Owen looks at me, confused. "What?" Chloe splashes him with more water, and he wipes his face, sighing. "Chloe, time out. I'm talking to Mommy."

"I'm going out. Just for a little," I say. "I wanted to grab a few things from the grocery store for tomorrow."

He tilts his head. "Can't you just do that

tomorrow?"

I roll my eyes. "Owen, I should be able to leave the house as well sometimes."

"But I have work tonight," he reminds me.

I nod. "I know. I'll be back before you get her to bed."

"Daddy's putting me to bed," Chloe shouts. "Yay!"

He smiles at the comment. "Okay," he says, looking back at me. "Try not to be too long though."

I nod. "Sure."

As I leave my house, I go over what he said to me just now.

"Try not to be too long."

Why? You don't want to miss out on more time with your girlfriend?

I know I need to plan things out. Be careful with what I do, but this needs to happen soon.

When I get inside the van, I reach over to the passenger side and look inside the hardware store bag. I stare at the duct tape and box cutter, wondering if this is really what I want to do.

CHAPTER 19

Emma

Owen will be coming over any moment now. He texted me a while ago to let me know. Part of me wishes he was here now to get our talk over with. Like a band-aid, I need to rip it off.

Is there someone else besides me? Who? If so, why? I thought we had something special.

I can already feel my nerves, or it may just be the five cups of coffee I've had today. For whatever reason, whenever I'm anxious, I crave caffeine more.

I made the mistake of taking another walk today, and when I passed by our coffee shop, I decided to go inside. Drinking alone at our place made me even more anxious.

It's like I'm already jumping to conclusions.

Why do I have to be so negative? There could be explanations for everything. There could really be a terrible roommate. There may be tensions at work. Those texts may be from his coworker. It could all be innocent, yet I'm treating it like anything but.

I can hear my sister in my ear as I sit on the couch in my apartment, aimlessly watching television. "There's another woman." Julie didn't say those words, but she said everything but. She wanted to be there for me, but I could hear her own mind fighting to tell me how stupid I am for believing Owen.

The day has dragged on and on. No matter how many times I've gone for a walk or how many hours of Netflix I've watched, waiting for my boyfriend to come is agonizing.

Despite that, I almost want to text him back and cancel. I don't feel well is the excuse I came up with. It's true. My stomach has been in knots all day. Maybe it's better not knowing the truth. Owen makes me happy, and I know I make him happy.

I don't need to know more than those facts to remain in the dream life Owen gave me since he entered my world.

A buzz in my apartment startles me at first. It's from the front door. Owen's finally here. Too late to text him now. I could put on my best acting skills like I did when I was a child and didn't want to go to school by pretending to be sick. A few fake coughs. Rubbing my hands and heating my forehead to make it feel unusually warm. I could demand a raincheck on this adult conversation.

I sigh, thinking what Julie would say when I tell her I put off talking to Owen. Despite being an annoying older sibling who thinks she's always right, sometimes I pretend she's with me when making hard decisions.

I open my apartment door, taking a few steps towards the front door. No rainchecks or fake coughs. I need to have this conversation. We need to sort our relationship out.

I want the truth.

When I open the door, I let out a laugh when I realize it's not Owen but a woman. In my daze at how my day's been, I nearly don't recognize her at first without her dark sunglasses.

"Hey," I say. "Karen, right?"

She smiles. "Hey, Emma. Yeah, Karen. I was the one who you tried to talk off the ledge the other day when I was having a breakdown outside your apartment." She lets out a nervous laugh. "Sorry, maybe this was a bad idea, but I was in the area again and thought of you."

"You did?" I say, surprised.

"Well, you were so nice the other day. I was having a rough time and you offered tea. If the offer is still there, I'd like that very much." She grins.

I take a deep breath. Owen could be coming by any moment. He's already late though. I know from past experience not to hold Owen to his word about when he may come by. He always has a last-minute showing or sales call he must get through. His job is such a grind. Some weeks he can be out all day while other times he's not doing much at all.

Anything is better than waiting for Owen to arrive. I feel like I'm going crazy sitting around.

"Sure, come in," I say. "That would be nice." I meet her smile with my own and gesture at her to follow me inside my apartment. She sits in the living room as I run through what choices I have. We both decided on matcha green tea.

"A little milk, please," Karen asks.

While the kettle's on the stove heating up, I sit across from her and smile. "I didn't expect you tonight," I say, looking around at the half-eaten pizza on the living room table. "Sorry."

She shakes her head. "No, please, I'm the one interrupting your day."

"Can I ask, what happened with your mom?" Instantly, I regret asking. Why do I start off with such an intrusive question? This is why I have no friends.

Karen gives a small smile. "Yeah, well, it was breast cancer. She found out too late. It was over five years ago now."

"Sorry," I say. "So, you're from Windsor originally?"

This is the type of question I likely should have started with. Not, hey how did your mom die, but where are you from? What do you do? All those small talk questions.

She nods. "Born and raised. How about you?"

"Originally from Toronto, but I moved out here with my sister."

"That's nice," Karen says.

"I sort of lived with her for a long time until just recently. I decided to move into the city. She's out in Essex County." I take a breath. "Was hoping for a new start in Windsor."

She smiles. "And how's that going so far?"

I nod and laugh. "Well, I'm not too sure, to be honest. Looking for employment is a little difficult at the moment, but I'm sure things will turn around. I hope."

"What about your love life? A pretty young woman like you must not have difficulty at all in that department." Karen smiles again, only this time there's something odd about her reaction. There's a tenseness in her face that doesn't match her calm demeanor.

I let out another laugh. "Well, that's also a little complicated."

"What?" Karen says surprised. "Why?"

"He's actually coming by pretty soon. You might meet him. I guess I'm worried. I know he loves me; I'm just worried about opening up to him."

I think about spewing everything out to Karen, despite only knowing her for a handful of minutes. Isn't that how people make friends though? Being vulnerable. I'm sure man trouble is something she can relate to.

When I look at her, she seems even more unsettled. She's wearing a tight, forced smile, her posture rigid, except for her leg that's crossed on her lap and fidgeting.

"Are you okay?" I ask.

She nods several times, maintaining a wide smile. "So, he loves you?"

I can't help but grin thinking of him. "Yeah, he does. He was about to tell me the other day, but I don't know. I'm just worried."

"Why are you worried?" she asks, slipping her hand in her purse.

It takes me a moment to answer. "I really love him." I give a thin smile to Karen and look down. I can hear her rummaging through her purse as I try and find the right words to explain myself. "I've never felt this way with a man before. It's hard to explain." I look at her. "What about you? Are you seeing someone?"

She shakes her head. "Well, I was, but like you, it's complicated." She grins. Again, her expression seems off. Maybe that's just how she is. I don't know her well to make such a judgement.

I realize this woman is in her own vulnerable place right now. After all, that's why I found her outside my doorstep, weeping. She's remembering good times with her mother. Being in a similar place, I know how difficult that is.

"I wanted to share something with you the other day," I say. "It's something we have in common."

"Oh," Karen says with a weird enthusiasm. "What could that be?" Her hand is still in her purse and I'm starting to wonder what she's attempting to find.

"Well, I lost my mom too. It's been nearly eight years for me. I think about her often though."

Karen's grin wanes, and she looks at me with a soft gaze, her rigid posture relaxing in front of me. Her hand comes out of her purse, gripping ChapStick. She applies it quickly to her lips before throwing it back in her bag and looking at me.

"I'm so sorry," she says. "I suppose we do have that in common. Can I ask what happened?"

I clear my throat. "Suicide." I take a deep breath and can feel a tear welling in my eye. I hate myself for this. I try to compose myself, and thankfully the sound of the kettle shrieking in the kitchen breaks the tension.

CHAPTER 20

Karen

I didn't think it was possible for me to find any empathy for my husband's mistress, yet when she spoke about her mother killing herself, something inside me switched. I went from a rageful wife to an empathetic stranger.

Suicide. How terrible.

The way Emma speaks about not having friends got to me as well. When I lied about being in her neighborhood because I was reminiscing about my own dead mother, Emma opened her door to me. Trauma over a deceased parent was something we shared.

Only her trauma is much more terrible than cancer. I'm curious why her mother killed herself but tiptoed around the subject.

Emma brings me a mug, and I thank her. I take a deep breath before continuing to talk about her mother. "That's awful," I say.

When my mother was dying from cancer, my family and I got to spend our last moments together in her hospital room. As terrible as that was, there was a shared love in the room that we got to have with my mom one last time. There was a beauty to it. We were all there for her in her last moments on Earth. That would certainly be the way I wish to die someday, surrounded by the people who love me.

A flicker of anger hits me as I think Owen would be one less person in that hospital room with me. Instead, he'd be off screwing about with the pretty woman in front of me.

I look down at my purse. Inside the large bag, I brought the duct tape and box cutter. It took all my energy not to slide the knife across her pretty little neck as she continued on about Owen. Every mention of their love brought my hand an inch closer to showing her the blade.

That's not how the Heartbreak Killer murders though. It would ruin everything I have planned.

"Was your mother sick?" I ask. I'm genuinely curious about what happened to her and why she ended her own life.

She shakes her head. "She went through a lot, my mother. Her love life was more than complicated. My dad was not an easy man to be with." Emma blows into her mug. "I think that's why I struggle with Owen."

"Owen," I say with a smile. "That's his name."

She shakes her head. "You know, I get so paranoid about sharing personal details, and yet with you it just comes out." She laughs. "I haven't even shared his name with my own sister." She takes a sip of tea and lowers her cup, looking at me intensely. "What would you do if you're not sure you can trust the man you're with?"

"You don't trust Owen?" I ask. This could be the second thing we share together.

She smiles. "I'm starting to think there could be another woman. I don't know."

For a moment, I think about telling her the truth about who I am. That's until she continues to open her mouth and more disgusting words come out.

She shakes her head. "I just want to be happy for once in my life, you know. So what if there's another woman? What if, I don't know, worst case he's married? Maybe he's on the outs with his nagging wife." She laughs.

I can feel my face drop as she talks. Realizing how upset I must look, I do my best to put on a grin as she continues to dig her own grave.

"I don't know," she says. "If there is another woman, maybe he's in the process of breaking things off with her."

I take a deep breath and take a sip of tea. The hot water burns my lips, but I hide the pain as I think about reaching back into my purse.

"Relationships are built on trust," I say, putting my mug on the coffee table. "If he's willing to break the trust he has in another relationship, why do you think you're so special that he won't do the same to you someday?"

She lowers her head. I may not have physically hurt her yet, but my words had an impact.

She looks at me with a small smile. "That's true. You know, you sort of remind me of my sister. You tell the truth. I think I'm just head over heels in love with the man; it's hard to think straight. I mean, he's perfect. Handsome. Smart. Funny. When I'm with him, I feel like I'm the only woman in the world he sees. I've never felt that way before. If he is cheating on me, it's hard to admit that I should give up those feelings because someday I'll be on the other end."

"Someday you will," I say confidently, looking into my purse. I see the edge of the duct tape roll inside.

Emma lets out a laugh. "Too much information, I know, but the man is really good in bed."

She laughs again and I pretend she's funny, even though I consider choking her. I don't let my dark thoughts take over. I calm my temper and stand up from the couch instead.

"Thanks so much for the conversation and tea," I say. "It was lovely to get to know you better."

"You haven't finished your tea," she says, surprised.

"Sorry. I have to get back home. I wasn't supposed to be out long."

"Well, we should do this again sometime," Emma says with a wide grin.

"I'm sure we'll see each other again soon," I say. I look around her apartment. "Can I use the washroom before I leave?"

She smiles and nods towards a closed door. "No problem."

Once inside the bathroom, I turn on the faucet as loud as it will go. Staring at myself in the mirror, I question what I'm doing.

I can hear my brain fighting with itself over what to do.

"She deserves it," a voice says. And I certainly agree with that.

"If you do this, there's no going back," a more reasonable voice shouts inside me.

All it takes is thinking of Emma's stupid laugh about how good of a screw my husband is for me to make my decision. I turn to the window and look outside the blinds. It leads directly out to the alley at the side of the building. I smile as I unlock the window. I attempt to open it and confirm I can before smiling at myself in the mirror again.

I can hear only the dark voice inside me now. "We'll see each other again real soon, Emma."

CHAPTER 21

Owen

It's past eight at night by the time Karen comes home. We barely talk as I rush out the door. Before leaving, I let her know that Daddy duties were completed.

Bath time with Chloe. Check.

Changed into pajamas. Check.

Snack. Usually, she eats something before bath and not bedtime, but she said her tummy was hungry and kept rubbing her belly near me until I made her food.

Karen thanked me and wished me the best with the late night showing.

I've had showings around this time before Emma came into the picture. It wasn't often, but it did happen. Of course, now that I'm seeing Emma, it's a lot more frequent. I know I can't get away with this much more, but tonight, it's worth it.

I'm almost certain Emma read the messages on my phone last night. While part of me thought about feigning being upset about my privacy being broken, I know if I want to keep this relationship strong, I can't keep lying. The more I build our relationship based on that foundation, the more doomed we are.

The question is, how can I tell her the truth? Not the whole truth, of course. If I do, I'm sure she'd leave me instantly. I couldn't handle that.

At least one complication in my life may have improved. Alexandria. She hasn't called or texted since we met in the parking lot this morning.

Besides meeting Emma, all I can think about was how I handled myself with Alexandria. I can still see her face, her eyes, as my hand gripped tighter around her neck.

It wouldn't have taken much for me to end that complication in my life entirely. After she threatened to tell my wife and daughter about our past affair, I couldn't think straight. Rage took over. A part of me I hadn't seen in a long time.

Her eyes haunted me all day. The expression on her face when she realized she could die.

I didn't like how that made me feel. I didn't like anything about how that went down.

There were opportunities for me to see Emma today. I was too worried about what Alexandria would do though. I must have driven past my own house nearly ten times today. I worried I'd find Alexandria outside on my lawn, peering through my windows at my wife and child. Or worse, knocking on the door and telling them everything.

She'd do that. She's absolutely insane.

But she's backed off, at least for now. No more harassing calls for the rest of the day. I'm sure that could change. Alexandria could be at my front door right now.

There's nothing I can do about that.

I can't put off speaking to Emma. I need to see her.

As I drive to her apartment, I attempt to calm and reassure myself that everything will be okay. I've managed all these complications in my life up till now, and I know there's a way to make everything I want to come true.

I can be with Emma. I can have Chloe. The two most important girls in my life will be with me.

As I got my daughter ready for bed, Alexandria's eyes haunted me. How can I be a good father when I almost killed a woman today? I try not to think of it. I need to focus on what matters. Emma.

As I get closer to her apartment, I worry how my conversation will go today. I'm always confident when I talk to people. It's a natural skill I have. An advantage that helps with my sales figures. Emma isn't buying a house. I'm trying to sell her me.

It's more personal. There's a lot of reasons why someone shouldn't be with me.

For a moment, I think of Karen and quickly force myself to focus on finding parking outside Emma's building. At this time of night and in this neighborhood, it's not exactly difficult. There's plenty to choose from.

With it being a rougher area, I tend to park as close as I can. I'm always hypervigilant around her neighborhood. When I park, I smile as I look at the building's front door. I know this conversation won't be an easy one to get through, but it's worth giving everything I have if it means being with Emma.

My smile wanes when I see movement in the alleyway. A crash of glass and tin catches my attention. I'm sure it's someone collecting beer bottles for cash but peer out of my car to make sure.

It's not what I expected.

A woman looks back at me, her face just as surprised as mine. She pushes her curly hair over her shoulder and turns and walks away from me into the dark alley.

Even in the dim light, I can make out Alexandria.

She knows about Emma? How? For how long?

I roll my window down. "Hey! Let's talk. Come back."

I look at the building. I was loud enough that if Emma had her window open, she could hear me. She'd for sure recognize my voice.

Alexandria doesn't stop and instead hurries down the alley. My body tightens and my hand grips the steering wheel. I'm squeezing it so hard that I feel I could rip it off. I put the car in drive and quickly make my way around the corner to cut her off. I park and hide near the exit of the alley, every so often peering around the corner.

Already, I can see her slim silhouette coming towards me. Every so often, she turns her head to look back from where I called out to her. She hasn't seen me yet, and I make sure to stay concealed. The smell of garbage from a Chinese restaurant dumpster keeps me company as I wait patiently for Alexandria to come into view. When she does, I jump out quickly, grabbing her with both hands.

"Let me go," she shrieks.

"Shut up!" I yell back. With one hand gripped on her forearm, I put a finger to my lip. "Stop yelling," I say in a calm voice.

I'm not sure if it's my face, which I'm sure is full of rage, or how tight I'm holding, but she gives me that look again. The same wide expression she had from earlier today.

I could have killed her in that parking lot. Part of me wonders if there were not so many cars driving by, if I would have released my grip from her throat.

Now, it's dark. We're concealed in an alleyway. Nobody is here.

I turn my head and look at the dumpster behind me, the smell of cold noodles still striking my nose.

When I look back at her, I do my best to lighten my features and calm myself. "What are you doing here?" I ask, not releasing her arm.

"You told me you couldn't be with me because you're married. Then I found out about this girl."

I shake my head. "How do you know about her?" Alexandria doesn't answer. I tighten my grip on her arm and force her closer. "How long have you been following me around?"

"Enough to know everything," she says with a devilish smile. "I know everything I need to ruin you."

"Alexandria," I say, taking a deep breath, "if you really cared about me, why would you want to hurt me like this?"

Her face drops, confused by what I'm asking. "You hurt me," she manages to say.

I look at her, taking in the wet eyes that no doubt will turn to full-on tears soon. I let go of her arm and take a step back. "I never wanted to hurt you. I just worried." As I think of the words to say next, I instantly regret that I didn't choose them better. "What we had was special. It was. I wasn't ready."

She huffs. "And you are ready now? You know I treat you better than her. She can't keep up with you like I can."

"I know," I lie. "Listen, I think of you often. Back when we were together, I worried what would happen if things didn't work out. I worried about us working together. I worried about everything. I didn't plan to move on to Emma. It just happened."

She smirks. "Is that her name? Emma?" She huffs again. "You know I'm better for you. Just break it off. You said you're ready now."

I know I'm stupid. What I'm telling Alexandria is

complete garbage, worse than what's in that dumpster. My hope was to persuade Alexandria to just let me go, but instead she wants me back. After what I did to her today, she still wants me.

She's insane.

I picture the expression her eyes made when my hand was wrapped around her neck. I look around the empty alley. All that's here is us. The dumpster is readily available and empty enough to put more inside.

I sigh. What do I have to do to get Alexandria to stop? How far must I take this before she listens? Whatever I'm saying here now isn't working.

I need to be more direct.

"Alexandria, I don't deserve you," I say. "Look at what I did to you this morning. That's not love. You deserve someone who loves you and won't hurt you. You need a better man than me."

I'm not sure what type of reaction my words will elicit. My hope is some form of agreement. That she will realize how right I am. If only she could read my mind right now, she'd understand how true I'm being.

Instead, her face sours. "I know what you're doing. You think you can use me, my body, tell me you love me, promise me the world and throw me away like garbage."

I turn and look at the dumpster again. I attempt to calm myself, but it's getting harder.

"I tell you what you don't deserve," she says, pointing a finger into my chest. "Your wife, your child, or your pretty girlfriend."

"Stop, Alexandria," I demand, taking a step towards her. "Just stop."

"Or what?" she says with a thin smile. "You'll hurt me again?" She turns and looks down the alley towards Emma's apartment. "You're not the only one who can hurt people."

Her words strike me, and I worry what they mean. Does she plan to physically hurt Emma?

I take a deep breath and find my next words carefully. "Please, let's cool off. Today has been a real emotional one. I never wanted to hurt you this morning, and I know you love me. I know that. I know you don't want to destroy me. Let's just take a breather. Let's take some time to think about what we have."

"You just want to go to your girlfriend's house," she says with a tone. "Emma." She says her name mockingly.

I shake my head. "I'm not. I'm going to go home. I won't see her. Promise me… you'll go home too. Let's not make this worse tonight. Let's both sleep on this, and we can talk more tomorrow. Is that okay?"

She pauses a moment and lowers her head. "Fine. But we need to talk tomorrow."

I nod. "Good. Promise me that you'll leave here though." When she nods back, I wonder if she's just as full of it as I am.

CHAPTER 22

Karen

Another late night showing with clients… Does he think I'm stupid enough to believe such a thing? Even if I didn't know the actual truth, I'd like to think I would have pieced his infidelity together easily. His lies are so shallow and obvious. Yet he brandishes his charming smile while telling me lie after lie, thinking his dumb wife doesn't know better. How narcissistic is he that he thinks nobody is onto what he is?

A cheater.

At one point, I saw my neighbors, Alice and Jason. They were in their living room, the blinds open. They had wine and I could hear the faint sound of music from my house as I watched them in the dark. At one point, I saw them slow dance. I must have watched them from my house for over thirty minutes, mesmerized by what a happy marriage could look like.

They looked so happy that it made me sick. Part of me wants to knock on their door and show them why there's nothing to be happy about in this world. It all goes to shit.

The more I think about my third interaction with Emma, the more I hate him. The more I hate her as well.

She actually said to my face, "Who cares if he's married?" Who in their right mind says such a thing? If only she knew who she was saying it to.

If only she knew what was in my purse.

I thought about ending it there. Taking out the knife and murdering her quickly. I'd have to apply the duct tape after she was killed though. That's not how the Heartbreak Killer works. I needed to remind myself to keep my cool.

The Heartbreak Killer had more fun with their victims. Binding them and taunting them before they killed.

I can see the appeal. I want nothing more than to end the pain I feel by taking out my anger and frustration on his pretty girlfriend.

Who cares if he's married? I let her words sink in, reminding me why I wanted to do this.

I felt pity and sadness for her after she mentioned her mother. I felt anger immediately after she said she planned to continue dating Owen even if he's married.

Which he is!

Poor Emma. I'm sure her sister will mourn her.

Who cares though? I twist Emma's phrasing to match my own attitudes about what I want to do.

But do I still want to do it?

I've been at home for over an hour now, sitting on the edge of my bed, trying to let my emotions direct my actions.

It's not working. My body is resisting.

Instead of putting Chloe to bed, I should have driven her to my dad's house for a late-night visit. I haven't figured out a reason for the emergency errand that I need my father to watch Chloe for. My hope was to figure out a reason for the last-minute visit on the way to my dad's, but my rage is blinding.

That and my hesitation.

He deserves what's coming. Owen's been asking for it for a long time. He thinks he can continue to ruin my life, talk to me like I'm stupid while he bangs his whore.

She deserves it too. Even if she doesn't know who I really am, she told me to my face the person she was. The kind who doesn't care if he's married.

She only cares about herself. About being "happy", she said.

Emma doesn't deserve happiness. She's a homewrecker.

Is she really though? She doesn't know for a fact that Owen is married or is seeing another woman. She could be just processing her own emotions. She fell for Owen's charms and lies, just as I had.

Can I blame her?

I cover my face and shake my head at my

indecision and inaction. If I really wanted to go through with what I want, why am I still sitting on my bed? The plan is easy. Too easy now that I've unlocked the bathroom window.

Go to her apartment. Open the window. Climb through. Wait until she's vulnerable.

Kill her.

When she's discovered, the symbol of the Heartbreak Killer will be found on her chest. Her arms duct-taped.

The Heartbreak Killer will have returned, only this time their identity will be easily identified. Owen. He's the killer. The evidence I plant will make it clear.

I stand up from the bed, letting the dark thoughts swirling inside me take me over. I leave the bedroom thinking of Emma's lifeless body and hate how much that makes me happy. I stop in my tracks at the sound of the front door opening.

Owen's home.

He left Emma's. Why? She mentioned things with him were complicated. Did something happen?

I imagine he dumped her. Speaking with her today, it's obvious she won't leave him. Suddenly, Owen's home early instead of spending all night in her bedroom.

For a moment, my heart flutters at the idea that I don't have to go through with what I planned. Is there a way I could forgive him?

Can I forgive Emma? I'm still rageful at the

thought of her.

What if this is my sign to let everything go? To not go through with what I planned?

When I think of our past, there's still so many positives in our relationship. First, there's Chloe. Our baby girl. When I was pregnant with her, Owen would go on multiple runs out of the house to fulfil any cravings I had, no matter the time. I remember how happy we were in our parenting courses we took when I was six months pregnant. He jokingly made a face when he changed the plastic baby's diaper. He made the exact same face when he changed Chloe when she was born, only this time it was genuine.

That Owen can still exist. The man I fell in love with. The man I married and who I planned to live forever with.

Owen walks up the stairs slowly and stops when he sees me leaning against the door of our bedroom.

"How'd it go tonight?" I ask him, hoping to see any indication in his words or reaction to gauge what happened with him and Emma.

He shakes his head, his face stoic. "Didn't make a sale," he says. He brushes past me into our bedroom, taking off his blazer and tossing it on the bed. I see his cell phone slip out of his jacket pocket, and for a moment, I think of grabbing it and searching through his messages. He unbuttons his shirt and gives me a thin smile. "Maybe tomorrow will be better."

"Maybe," I say, hoping that's the truth. Before I can say another word, he stretches.

"Going to be long day tomorrow," he says. "I've got that stupid meeting Doug is forcing us all to attend. Some soft skills course on how to active listen. He thinks it will improve relationships with our clients. It's a big waste of time and it will take up my entire office day." He yawns. "Plus, the couple wants to think about the house some more. I may have another late showing with them tomorrow night if they change their mind. Is that okay?" He looks at me with his bright eyes, expecting his stupid wife to agree. "The only time they can meet is late. She's a nurse with crazy hours and he works days."

I pause in awe of his ability to pull fake realities out of his ass so easily. "What does he do for a living? The husband?" I ask him to dig his grave deeper.

He takes a deep breath and looks up. "I think he said he's a teacher, or something like that."

I smile. "Well, maybe you'll close the deal tomorrow."

I think I've found my muse for going through with my own plans. My smile widens as I watch him get changed into a white shirt and shorts for bed.

"What is it?" he says with a raised eyebrow.

"Oh, nothing," I say, but I can't help my thoughts as they play out what it will look like someday when my husband changes into orange shirts and loose joggers. When he goes to jail, he'll spend many nights playing back in his mind how he got caught.

As we slip in bed, he pecks me on the lips before turning off the nightlight. "Night," he says, turning over.

He looks away from me, and I stare at the back of his head, wondering how easy it would be for me to grab the lamp and bash him with it.

What I have planned is more devious, as methodical and awe inspiring as his ability to lie. My husband has a skill. Lying. Soon, he'll discover what my talents are.

As I hear his breathing slow, he turns towards me in some state of sleep. My anger softens as I look at my handsome husband, facing me in our marriage bed.

It doesn't have to be this way. I can stop myself from making this worse.

Then I think of Emma, and it all comes crashing down. The only thing that makes me happy is knowing what will happen next time I'm at her door.

I take a deep breath, looking at my husband. My face distorts to reveal the rage inside me. "I hate you," I whisper to him.

CHAPTER 23

Emma

After all the back and forth on wanting to see Owen last night, he made the decision for me.

"I'm not feeling well," his text read. "Can we meet up tomorrow?"

Of course I responded yes, but it was at that moment I realized how much I wanted to get it over with. I had to spend another night wondering what's happening in the relationship with the man I love.

Love.

I actually love him. I know because of how hurt I feel. My stomach has been in knots all night and this morning. I'm so overwhelmed with emotions.

Owen said he'd come by later after work. He has some mandatory sales meetings all day.

Although I know I'll see him soon, the buildup is dreadful. I could puke just thinking about how many more hours I need to wait to see him.

For once in my life, I thought I was happy. I

thought I'd found the perfect man. I had such high hopes for what being with Owen could bring to my life. Stability, romance, and more than that, a friendship that could last forever.

I think of my sister and her husband. Living in their basement, I know their love life isn't perfect, but somehow I know that they'll always be together.

David is such a pragmatist. He doesn't let arguments get out of hand, and you can tell how much he loves my sister. Pictures of them throughout their relationship are scattered around every room in their house, even in the basement where I dwelled.

I hated staring at the picture of them in my basement room. It was taken on their honeymoon in Rome. I'd look at it often, wondering if I'd ever find anything where I could be half as happy as Julie is with David.

I thought about taking down the picture, but of course it wasn't my house.

Thinking of Julie, I know I should probably call her back. She's called several times this morning. I haven't picked up.

I know what she wants.

Updates. How did it go with my mystery man last night. She'll want to know, and I wish I had answers.

As if wanting to torment myself more, I dial her number on my cell. She picks up quickly.

"Hey," she says. "Are you okay? Did it go bad last night?" There's a long pause before she continues. "Sorry,

I was just worried about you."

"He didn't come last night," I say, lowering my head and sitting on the couch. "He said he wasn't feeling good."

"Ugh," my sister groans, feeling my frustration. "We should follow him or something. Maybe you can figure out what's happening that way."

I nearly smile when she says "we". She really does have my back.

"I don't want to be that kind of girlfriend," I say, taking a deep breath. "Besides, he says he's coming over tonight."

"What are you going to do if it's the worst case with him? If he's with someone else?"

I lower my head. "I don't know."

"Well—"

"Julie," I say with a harsh tone, "stop. I know you mean well, but I'm just having a hard time. I don't know what I'll do or how I'll respond." I think of that picture of David and Julie in the basement and can feel a tear welling in my eye. I hate how emotional this is for me. I hate waiting for Owen for answers. "I just want to be happy… like you."

There's a long pause on the phone before Julie responds. "It's going to be okay, Emma. You don't need a man to be happy in life."

I sigh. "That's easy to say when you're happily married with a beautiful child and a large house. White picket fence and all the stereotypes of what a dream life looks like."

Wasn't my dream life supposed to start with Owen?

There's another pause before Julie says a word. "You're not drinking again, are you? It's okay if you are, I just want you to be honest with me."

I shake my head even though she can't see me. "No, I'm not. I promise on everything that means the world to me. I promise on Rowan I'm not drinking."

"Stop, Emma," she pleads. "I don't like it when you talk like that. You shouldn't swear on my son."

"I just want you to believe me when I say it this time," I say. There were many times when she did and I lied. There are many things I regret lying about. "I really thought I had something special with him."

"Well, you still haven't talked to him. Maybe there's an explanation. Maybe something else is going on. You don't have to jump to the worst case before talking to him."

I don't respond, because I know the answer. My life is terrible. I'm terrible. I'll never be happy because I don't deserve it.

I let out a sigh. If I'm right and there is another woman, I don't know what I'll do. I feel like I'm going insane just waiting for Owen to see me.

"Maybe I should just go back to your house," I say, giving up. "Maybe that's where I'm supposed to be in life."

"Emma, stop," she pleads again. "You deserve to be happy. You deserve to find someone who loves you, but you don't need to force it. Someday, that person will come into your life. I promise you."

I let her words sink in. Before I can say anything else, the buzzer goes off.

"What's that sound?" Julie asks.

"It's the front door," I say. "Someone's buzzing my apartment. Hold on."

I leave my apartment and open the front door. My phone nearly drops out of my hand when I see who it is.

CHAPTER 24

Owen

I smile when Emma opens the door. When she greets me back with a thin, cautious smile, my worst fears are confirmed.

"I have to let you go," she says and puts her phone in her pocket. She looks at me and I know something is wrong.

"I brought coffee," I say. "From our place. A venti blonde vanilla latte. I probably got something wrong, but this is the best I can do."

I stretch out my hand, the warm coffee heating my palm. She doesn't take it immediately, but reluctantly does. "You messed up a little. A venti iced half-sweet blonde vanilla latte. Close enough." She looks at me, pursing her lips. "Are you feeling better today?" She examines my face like an FBI investigator questioning a killer.

I shake my head. "Not really, and I can't stay and talk. I just wanted to come by to start my day nicely by seeing you." She doesn't respond. I lower my head.

"You saw the text messages on my phone the other day, didn't you?" There's no point in pretending otherwise. She slowly nods. "I know we have a lot to talk about," I say, "and I have some things to explain to you. I'll go over everything with you, okay?"

"I just want to know the truth, Owen," she says. "That's all I care about."

I nod. "And you deserve it." I look around outside. "I'll come back as soon as I'm done at work. We can go over everything together." Out of the corner of my eye, I see someone walking down the street. I turn to make sure it's not her. Emma looks too.

Once I confirm it's not Alexandria, I turn back to Emma with a thin smile, trying my best to convey in my facial reactions how I'm feeling. "It's just important for me to tell you before we meet again tonight that you know how much I love you, Emma."

She lowers her head. "Owen—"

I wave my hand in my defence. "I'll explain everything, but you need to know that. I love you, Emma. I love everything about you. All I want to do is spend every moment with you for the rest of my life."

Suddenly, a grin appears across her beautiful face, and I smile back. I could jump up and down in joy at how great I feel at this moment. It's not how I wanted to say it, but I needed to before I see her tonight.

"Owen, I can't say that back right now," she says. "We need to talk tonight."

I nod and grin. "I know we do, and I have a lot to

say." My eyes meet hers, and all I see is the love she has for me that her lips won't say. "See you soon."

It takes everything for me not to lean in and kiss her. It's all I want in the moment, but it doesn't feel right.

Instead, I leave, looking back once to make sure she's watching me. She is. I turn and get into my car, taking a moment to stare at her again. She's leaning against her apartment door, watching me as I leave.

My heart flutters inside my chest.

I know that no matter what happens, we can survive this. I just have to figure out how.

As I drive towards my office, I go over tactics on how I can get out of this in one piece. Alexandria knows about Emma. She knows where she lives.

How long has she been stalking us? How long until she stops hiding? When that happens, what will Alexandria do?

The obvious answer is she'll tell Emma everything.

Or worse. I remember what Alexandria said to me last night. *"You're not the only one who can hurt people."*

What did that mean?

Is she planning on hurting Emma? I should have collapsed her lung the other night and be done with her. No more problems. No worries about what she might say if she can never say another word.

I hit my steering wheel in frustration, the blow causing my horn to squeak. The driver in a Jeep in a lane beside me turns and gawks at me. Part of me wants to flip him off in response, but instead I try my best to calm myself.

Deep breaths. Get it together, Owen.

I woke up several times last night worried about what would happen after I left my house. What if Alexandria's knocking on Emma's door? What if she stayed outside her apartment building, stalking her? She promised she would leave, but did she? Is Emma safe? What was she planning to do?

If I didn't leave last night, I know Alexandria would have done something crazy. I had to go home or else things would have escalated.

I needed to ensure Emma was safe though. I drove by her house twice this morning, once just to ensure Alexandria wasn't there.

Just like me, she has to attend the presentation today. Apparently, my boss thinks we all need to "active listen" better. Even though she's our receptionist, every employee is required to attend.

Seeing that the presenter will start in the next ten minutes, I know she'll be at work. Now was a safer time to sneak away and see Emma. I needed to make sure she was okay. I couldn't start work without seeing her. I also needed to know if Alexandria spoke to her last night.

When Emma opened the door, I feared the worst. That she'd met with my ex-girlfriend. That she knew about Karen. She knew everything.

That's not the case, at least for now, but I know something is going to happen soon. The question is, how much do I tell Emma? A crazy ex-girlfriend could be easy enough to explain. My life with the other woman who shares my bed may be harder to swallow.

I arrive at work with only a minute to spare before the presentation begins. When I enter the building, Alexandria isn't at her desk. Nobody is at their desks though. Everyone is inside the meeting room. The presenter, a woman whose name escapes me, clears her throat and greets the room.

When I walk inside, the presenter greets me, and I apologize for being late. When I look around at my smiling coworkers, who quietly greet me with nods, only one person is noticeably missing.

Alexandria isn't in here.

My mouth drops open, and I do a double take to make sure I'm not going crazy. When I confirm that she's not amongst the others, I quickly turn and head out of the room without saying a word.

I look down the hallway at the women's washroom. She could be there. Don't panic, I tell myself.

I should be worried though. I'm staring at her empty desk when a hand lands on my shoulder. I quickly shrug it off and turn.

My boss, Doug Hinchers, looks at me oddly. "Easy, Owen," he says with a laugh. "We're about to start."

I look at him wide-eyed. "I can't stay. I have a big sale, that old Victorian-style downtown that I have. It needs some work."

He nods. "I know, Owen. You always have a

pending sale happening, but I need you to stay for this. This class is important for the company. I know it's the full day and that's a lot, but this is mandatory, so." He gestures towards the room. "Everybody is in the same boat as you."

Doug is the most stubborn man I know. Fighting this won't work. The only thing that can do is curse him out and quit on the spot.

I can't do that either.

I look at Alexandria's empty desk again. "Where's Alexandria today? I needed her to help on something."

Doug purses his lips. "Called in sick today." He looks at the meeting room. "Let's not keep the team waiting for us, Owen." He touches my shoulder and gently guides me to the meeting room as I stare at Alexandria's desk.

CHAPTER 25

Karen

When I pull into my dad's driveway, he's on his porch, sipping a beer, waiting for us. It's a little past noon and an odd time to be drinking, especially when he's watching my child.

Chloe doesn't notice my observation and instead squeals with joy and yells out, "Grandpa," even though he can't hear her. He does seem to notice her enthusiasm and waves at us in the van with a wide grin.

"Thanks again, Dad," I say as I step out and open the passenger side door for Chloe. She immediately runs up to my dad and bear hugs him with her petite arms. He laughs.

"Hey, Chloe," he says. "How's it going?"

"Can we watch cartoons again?" Chloe says, not answering his question.

He smiles. "Of course."

"I shouldn't be too long," I tell him. I'm about to leave when he again calls out for me.

Not today. I don't want to do this with him again. I don't have the patience for it. I need to be leaving. There are things I need to do before I go to Emma's place.

This time he doesn't wait for Chloe to go inside before he starts with the questions. "Where are you going today?" he asks.

There was a time when I could get away with "hey, Dad, can you watch Chloe for a few hours" without many follow-up questions.

"Just some errands, Dad," I answer, trying my best to stay cool.

"What are they?" he asks. Chloe tilts her head and stares up at me.

"I just need some time to myself. Is that okay?"

"It's been a lot lately, Karen," he says. Now he looks down at Chloe. "Go on. The remote is on the living room table." Chloe gives me a hug before heading inside.

Dad hasn't taken his eyes off me. "I know you said nothing's wrong, but a parent knows when their kid is up to something."

I want to lose it. Shout at him. How dare he question me? Maybe I should tell him the truth.

"Dad, I have murderous intentions today, and I need your help. Watch my kid."

It's his fault I'm this way. His anger seeped from his genetics into mine. Or maybe it was the years of seeing how he treated my mom that made me this way. This angry person tainted by hatred and with a hair trigger at all times.

I realize I can't get into a fight with my alibi though. I'll need him to stand by my version of what happens today.

I cover my face. "I don't know," I say. "Things have been… not the best with Owen."

"I knew it," he says, taking a sip of his beer. "What did he do?" For a moment, I see a flicker of rage across his eyes. The look I saw when I was a kid. I almost feel afraid looking at him now. Only I'm much braver now. He'd be the one scared of me if he knew what I was doing.

"Nothing, Dad," I say. "We're just in a bad place, I think." I sigh. "I can't believe I'm going to tell my dad this, but we haven't been intimate in months. I've been going for a lot of walks and runs lately. I'm trying to lose some weight."

His face drops, and so does his arm and beer. "I'm sorry," he says. "You're beautiful, Karen. Don't think you need to do anything for a man to love you."

I let out a laugh. I don't know what's funnier, the support my dad is showing me that I never ever anticipated him being emotionally capable of or his good advice.

"I just want to feel better," I say. "I've been working on myself."

He looks at me a moment, examining me, until he raises his beer and grins. "Well, I'm sure you know your mom and I could really go at it at times."

That's not how I remember it. More like he'd lose

his temper and shout and scream at Mom until she cried. I don't say that to him though.

"I know," I say instead. "I'm going to go now, Dad. Are we okay?"

He grins. "Of course. You can always bring Chloe over. Something that helped your mom and I was going out for dates. Maybe you should do that more. Of course Chloe can stay here. Maybe even a sleepover. Give Mommy and Daddy a night to themselves." He raises his eyebrows playfully.

I sigh. I wish this entire conversation never happened. "Thanks, Dad."

"Take your time going out," he says. "If you want today to turn into a sleepover, let me know."

As I leave and drive away, I think about what he said. Date nights probably wouldn't have been a bad idea. They likely could have helped. That was before my husband decided to put his dick in another woman.

Now there's only one way my marriage ends.

Before driving to Emma's house, I stop at a costume store I looked up online. It's the only place that offers year-round costumes to buy or rent.

Today, I'm dressed in different dark clothes, and I wanted to compliment my new attire with fake hair. Blond. Ironic since that's what Owen prefers in women. It's the same hair color his dear Emma has. If anyone notices me, it will be the hair color they see. I brought red lipstick as well. Another distraction to throw off my identity.

Before leaving the party store parking lot, I put on the wig and apply the lipstick carefully using the rearview mirror.

Now that I'm ready, I drive to Emma's apartment. The entire way there, I expect my conscience to get the better of me. Change my mind on what I want to do. Hear the little angel in my head fight with the devil over what course of action to take.

It's strangely quiet in my mind. It's as if my body is ready to take this to the next level.

I start by driving by Emma's apartment. As if it's a sign to go through with my plan, Emma walks out of her building, shutting the door behind her. She even pulls on the door to ensure it's locked.

Thankfully, that's not how I'll be getting into her apartment.

She looks toward my car, and I lower myself in my seat, looking at the road. When I pass her, I check my rearview mirror before finding a place to park.

CHAPTER 26

Emma

It seems like the past few days all I've been doing is waiting for answers. It's infuriating. After Owen visited me this morning, it's even worse.

Those three words can bring so much happiness and, in my case, confusion.

I love you.

It should be such a touching moment. The man I love told me he loves me. But the anvil is close above my head I can almost feel it. He's already admitted he's hiding something.

What is it? Another woman? Married? I don't know but it's driving me insane.

At first, I was so happy when he said the words, but now I wish he'd never come. I'd rather he came after work and explained it then. The waiting is difficult and it's all I've been doing.

Is this even worth it?

Deep down, I know the answer: yes. No man has

ever made me feel this way. I never felt as certain in my life that I was made for another as much as I felt with Owen. My sister said that Owen may not be my person but how can that be if he's the only one who has had this power over me?

Just like yesterday, I've been going for many walks. Eating garbage food while garbage daytime television keeps me company.

With my head in the clouds, I leave my apartment building. Worried that I left the front door unlocked, I double check and out of habit, I've locked it.

It's going to be hours before I see Owen and it's too much to handle. I wish I could press fast forward on my life until I get to see him.

What is happening in my life? What is Owen hiding?

I turn down the block and head towards a park. I try to let the beautiful foliage and summer annuals calm my anxiety but stumble over my own feet. I nearly lose my balance but catch myself. When I look down, I see the culprit is a loose shoelace. One that I likely didn't even bother tying before I left my house. I need to get out of this daze. I need my life to get some clarity and soon.

I bend over to tie my shoe properly and notice a woman wearing dark clothes halfway up the block behind me. She stares at me and stops in her tracks, taking out her phone and leaning against a nearby tree. She brushes her curly blond hair over her shoulder.

I stand up and take a deep breath. Owen has my mind running in circles so I feel the need to go faster.

I break out into a light jog, making my way down the path. A few blocks away is the river. I love being near it. Across it is Detroit, Michigan. I've only been to the States a handful of times, but I love looking across the rough waters and knowing that another country is staring back at me.

As I make it to the path along the river, I take in the marvelous views. The river itself glistens as the sunlight dances on its surface.

I always wonder what Americans think when they look across the river at Windsor. We don't have a quarter of the tall buildings they have downtown, but it's green and spacious here. One of the few larger buildings they likely see is our casino, where Americans can cross a bridge and gamble at eighteen instead of twenty-one.

Nearly out of breath, I stop to take a break, leaning against the black iron fence, staring out over the Detroit River at America, watching the specks of people and cars on the other side.

An elderly couple walks slowly pass me. I smile when I recognize them. It's the same couple I saw at the coffee shop when I was waiting for Owen. There's something about watching them that makes my heart melt.

I could have that with Owen. I know it. Whatever he has to say, there's a chance we can still be together.

He may have some explaining to do, but if I think he's worth it, we can make it work. I imagine the old couple are retired together and take long walks by the river with multiple small dates at coffee shops along the way.

It's a beautiful thought.

Breaking my image of what a wonderful life with Owen could be like, I notice the woman in dark clothes again. She's walking up the path towards me.

I shake the weird thoughts I have and instead look back out towards Detroit.

Many people use the paths along the river to walk, run or bicycle. The woman likely lives downtown as well. But I can't shake the strange feeling.

I continue to walk down the path. The other day I walked all the way up to Ambassador Bridge. Today, I want to go the other way and see how far I can go before wanting to turn back.

When I start to walk, I turn and see the woman in dark clothes doing what I was doing a moment ago. Enjoying the view of the water and the city beyond. I walk past her and nod and greet her. She looks back at me and obviously notices me but says nothing. Instead, she turns her head and looks back out towards the water.

After thirty minutes of a mix between a light jog and a brisk walk, I've walked well past the casino and away from most people.

I smile when I realize I've accomplished my mission of not thinking about Owen. Of course, after that realization, he's all I can think about.

I walk down a small hill towards a path off the pavement. It's a trail that not many people walk. In fact, last week I found a small homeless encampment around here. When I walked by recently, they'd moved but some of their belongings stayed behind. A sheet over some trees for shade and some empty bottles.

I walk through the trees and up to the shore. It's rocky, and the fast-moving Detroit River brushes up the rocks beside me.

I smile when I get the idea to take off my shoes and socks and put my feet in the cool water. I haven't done this in a long time. I stuff my socks in my shoes and tip a toe in to test how cold it is. The summer is nearly over, but the humidity is still here. The cool waters are welcoming to my warm skin.

I hear the sound of a twig snapping and turn my head. A tree shuffles and I see a woman appear. It's the same one from before.

I thought when I saw her, she was older. It was hard to tell with her dark glasses and clothing. Up close, I can see how smooth her skin is and her long blond curls. For a moment, I think I know her.

"Who are you?" I ask, knowing that it can't be a coincidence that she's here. She followed me, but why?

I left my handbag on the rocks out of reach from where I am. My knife is there. I call out to the woman again, who just stares at me.

My heart beats faster as I realize this mysterious woman may mean me harm. She puts her hand into her pocket, taking her time. My eyes widen as I wonder if I should run for my bag or try to swim away.

Instead, I just watch her in horror as to what she'll

do next. She pulls out her cell phone and points it towards me, pushing on her screen before lowering her phone and staring at me again.

Then she turns and leaves.

I watch in confusion as the strange woman goes back up the path and out of sight.

CHAPTER 27

Owen

The day is ticking by slower. It's not just that the mandatory presentation is boring. Even if my mind wasn't elsewhere, I'd have a hard time caring what the presenter was saying.

We've had one break, and my boss, Doug, asked some of us what we thought so far. A few colleagues nodded their heads, and one kiss-ass mentioned that the soft sales skills they were learning could be really helpful with an open house they have next weekend.

I wanted to roll my eyes at the thought that anybody could get much use out of this. Of course, when I tried to leave again, Doug stopped me. This was required.

I wish I'd had the common sense to call in sick.

Every so often, I peer outside the meeting room towards reception, hoping to see Alexandria come in. I know that won't happen.

The real question I have is where is she? She's not sick. I know that much. There was no cough or sneeze coming from her when I caught her stalking my girlfriend.

No, she's not at home, sick. She's too busy ruining my life.

That narrows it down to two places: my house near my wife or near my girlfriend's apartment.

During the break, I even attempted to call Alexandria, but now it was her ignoring me.

"Where are you?" I texted her. "Are you really sick? Please don't do anything! I mean it!"

My blood boils as the presentation starts up again and I'm forced to sit in a room listening to some woman blab on about how to listen better.

As the presenter talks, my phone goes off. I apologize as I silence it. I don't hide that I'm looking at my cell out of instinct as I'm about to slide it back in my pocket.

We're realtors. We live and die with our phones in our hands. It shouldn't make a difference even though I see Doug giving me a stare that suggests he's not happy.

It's a text back from Alexandria. "I saw you today on your private coffee date with her. Maybe I should have some quality time with Emma as well. What do you think?"

My eyes widen and I quickly start to tap on my screen furiously. "Alexandria! Leave her alone! Don't—"

Doug whispers at me, "Put it away, Owen. You can talk to clients after."

I ignore him completely and attempt to finish my

text when a picture pops onto my screen. It's Emma. She's standing in water, looking at the camera. Her face says it all. She's confused and scared.

My mouth drops open. Alexandria is near her right now. She's in danger. And I'm learning active listening skills.

I stand up abruptly, causing the presenter to stop talking. The boss stands from his chair as well, his hands up as he's no doubt upset with me.

"I can't stay, Doug," I say with a harsh tone. "It's personal. I need to go."

"Owen!" Doug shouts as I leave the room and run out the front door, passing Alexandria's empty desk.

CHAPTER 28

Karen

I've been standing in the dark for what feels like hours. In real time though, it's been nearly thirty minutes.

Thirty minutes of going over in my head what will happen when Emma walks through her front door. Once she's comfortable in her apartment, I'll make my presence known. Part of me is excited to see her expression when I come out of her closet.

I run through different scenarios in my head. In some, Emma overpowers me. In most cases I get the upper hand.

I grip the box cutter in my hand, slipping the blade in and out with my thumb. I take a deep breath thinking about how it will feel when the knife cuts her skin.

This will work out perfectly. I'll take care of Emma, plant the evidence, and leave. I'll need to hurry back to my father's house as quickly as I can, ensuring I don't get caught when I leave the apartment building through the bathroom window.

The disguise will help with that.

Once at my dad's, despite the hard part being done, my day won't be over. Establishing an alibi isn't easy. I'll need to seem normal, which may be hard to do when adrenaline is shooting through me.

Eventually, my dear husband will come to his precious Emma, only to find her indisposed. Her pretty face won't be recognizable.

All the attractive qualities Emma has, I'll take away from her.

I'll call Owen's office closer to when he'll get off work. I'll try my best to time a phone call to 911 too. I'll use an outside line to do it. Pretending to be someone close to the crime scene, I'll say I heard a commotion in Emma's apartment building.

With any luck, the police will catch Owen red-handed in her apartment. I imagine him crying over the bed, where I'll place her body, and the police storming inside and arresting him immediately.

Even after his arrest, my work won't be done. I'll have to continue the act longer. The Heartbreak Killer will have returned, and Owen will be the main suspect.

He's not the Heartbreak Killer of course, but that doesn't matter. He'll be connected to the killer forever. Instead of asking if Owen is innocent of killing his mistress, the media and court of public opinion will be questioning if he's the notorious serial killer or just a copycat.

No matter which answer the actual courts arrive

at, the speculation will be out forever whether my husband is the Heartbreak Killer.

I'll have my alibi with my father. I'll have my life intact.

Owen will be in jail, likely for the rest of his life. He'll rot in a cell knowing his beloved Emma is dead, and he'll be prosecuted for her murder. For the remainder of his pathetic life, he'll be wondering what actually happened to Emma. Who killed her?

Poor Emma. She misses her mother deeply. I'll help reunite them.

I love everything about my plan. It oozes with the type of irony that I can't help but smile at when I think about.

Once the world sees the true monster my handsome husband really is, I'll leave him. Divorce. It will be easy and understandable.

It will be expected by everyone.

Chloe will see her daddy for the scum he is. We'll move on with life together, finding a better path for both of us. Owen and his lies will never follow us again.

Sure, he may suspect that perhaps his dumb wife, who he thought believed his lies, had a part in her murder.

My father will back up that we spent the whole night playing cribbage and watching cartoons with Chloe. Yes, I went for a run on my own, but that was in a park, where there's no cameras and fewer witnesses to prove that I was there.

After doing the deed, I can even go to the park and leave my car in the lot for a little while.

The only problem with my plan is that Emma is late for her own death. I knew she'd be out for a while, but my hope was that it would be a short walk around the neighborhood.

I take a deep breath, standing in her dark storage closet. I lean against the wall, tapping the box cutter against my black pants. Whatever fabric the blond wig is made out of is irritating my skin. Part of me wants to take off my disguise.

The more sinister side of me smiles when I think about Emma's face when I swing the closet door open and run at her with my knife. She won't expect it, and she won't register what's happening. Who is this woman with blond hair and bright red lipstick coming at her? Is that a large knife in her hand? What's happening?

Before she can register much, my blade will enter her, and soon it will all be over.

My cell rings in my pocket and I quickly silence it. Stupid. How dumb can I be? With my adrenaline rushing, I manage to put my phone on silent.

I look at the cell and see it's Dad. "Chloe wants to know if we can do a sleepover. What do you think?"

Well, I'd rather not. I need to spend time with him at his house afterwards but would rather decompress from tonight at my own house after I kill Emma, alone.

Breaking me from my thoughts, I hear footsteps coming from outside Emma's apartment. The door opens, and the steps are closer to me now. I can hear Emma flinging her car keys and taking off her shoes. She audibly sighs to herself as she moves around her apartment.

I try my best to barely breathe and make little to no movement. When I realize she's not as close to me, I drop my cell back in my pocket and grip my knife tightly.

CHAPTER 29

Emma

Who was the woman in black who followed me?

It's all I can think about as I make my way back to my apartment. I've never seen her before. For a moment, because of the dark sunglasses, I thought of Karen. My new friend, I suppose I'd define her as. I'm not sure if tea once at my place makes us buddies. I didn't even get her phone number. I only realized after she left in a hurry.

Hopefully she comes back. She said she would. It would be nice to make a friend in the city.

The woman who followed me was no friend, and she definitely wasn't Karen. Her blond curly hair gave that away.

Whoever she was, she targeted me for some reason.

How long had she been following me? I first saw her on a path leading to the river. Then at the river and finally off the path near the shore. Once she had me alone, she took my picture.

Another question I've been thinking about as I walk home. Why did she take a picture?

My paranoid self is starting to take over. I'm not safe. The woman could already know where I live. She could be waiting for me when I get home.

Why the picture though? What does the mysterious woman have in store for me next? From the manic smile she had on her face when she took my picture, I know it's not anything good.

I can't stay in this city. It's time to leave. I'm not safe here.

I think of Owen. He could always visit me in the country. We could still be together. It's going to be hours until he comes to my place though. Am I even safe in my own apartment while I wait for him to arrive?

After the incident with the stranger, I took out my pocketknife to make sure it's ready to use if I'm attacked on the way home. It takes much longer to get back to my apartment. I take a weird way home, zigging and zagging down different blocks, ensuring nobody was following me.

Knowing that I'm getting too paranoid, I finally go back to my apartment. I quickly open the front door, ensuring I lock it behind me. I take a deep breath, wishing I lived in an apartment building that has a peephole to look outside. The woman in black could be outside my building right now.

When I enter my apartment, I fling my keys across the room to the couch in frustration. I quickly take off my shoes and lower my blinds, peeking outside as I do. It feels like the world is out to get me suddenly and all I want to do is hide... and be with Owen.

The question is, how safe am I if I stay here? Does the woman know where I live? Is she outside right now?

Panicked, I grab my knife from my purse and hold it tightly to my chest, letting its small blade comfort me.

My apartment ringer buzzes, and I let out a shriek, unable to keep my tension inside me. The buzzer rings a second time. From my apartment, I don't have a view of the front of the building. I think about climbing through my window and escaping to the alley outside.

She's outside my door right now. I look at my knife and take a deep breath.

I have no reason to be afraid. This woman doesn't know who she's messing with. I storm up to the front door and open it quickly.

CHAPTER 30

Owen

When Emma opens her front door, I can't help but smile. A sense of relief washes over me. "Thank god," I say, not able to contain my feelings.

"Owen," she says, a hand behind her back. "I thought you were coming later."

I look around outside her building. The only person I see is a disheveled man rolling a shopping cart on the other side of the street. I notice a thick tree in the courtyard of the building. I feel like I've never noticed how large it is, and for a moment, I worry Alexandria could be behind it.

When I look back at Emma, she stares at me, confused.

"I needed to see you," I say. "It couldn't wait any longer." I look around outside again, ensuring she's not nearby. If Alexandria was crazy enough to corner Emma, what else is she willing to do?

Then it hits me. What if Alexandria already spoke to Emma? What if she's inside her apartment right now?

"Are you alone?" I ask her.

"Yeah," she says quickly. "Of course."

"Good," I respond, glancing at my car. "We should leave. I want us to talk, but not here."

When I look back, Emma's face sours. It's as if she can read my mind and knows the terrible things are there that I've been hiding.

"Is this about the woman I saw?" Emma asks.

I take a deep breath. Alexandria took her picture. But she must not have said much since Emma still has no clue who she is. Was Alexandria just trying to scare her, and me, by sending a picture of Emma to my cell?

Mission accomplished. Alexandria has my attention, which is all she seemingly wants for now. I know that this won't end with her cornering Emma and scaring her with photos.

It's not safe at Emma's apartment right now.

"Let's just go," I say. "I'll tell you everything, but I need you to trust me." I stare at her, our eyes meeting. I hope she can see how true my words are. She needs to believe me. Staying at her apartment is dangerous. After catching Alexandria outside the other night, I should have come clean then. I went home and left Emma in danger. I was worried to tell the truth, but if I don't now, Emma could get hurt. I couldn't live knowing that my actions caused that to happen.

She needs to leave. I'll drag Emma out of her place if she doesn't come with me willingly.

After a moment, her eyes soften, and she nods. "Okay," she says. "I'll go with you."

CHAPTER 31

Karen

What. The. Hell.

CHAPTER 32

Owen

As we drove through her neighborhood, I looked around cautiously for any sign of Alexandria. I peered down alleys, my head on a swivel for any sightings of my crazy ex-girlfriend.

Emma asked what was happening and I told her I'd explain everything once we were safe.

"Safe?" she repeated, shaking her head. "What have you gotten me into, Owen?"

What have I done, indeed.

It all stemmed from my lies. It all came from my complete mess of a life. It was stupid of me for thinking I could ever be with someone like Emma in the first place. For ever thinking I should be allowed to be happy. To have something that made sense, instead of the complicated life I've been living.

Emma was quiet until we pulled into the lot of the Sleepaway Motel, a long, low structure that looks like it hasn't had a fresh coat of paint in decades. A large, blinking neon sign advertised the pool and hourly rates.

Hourly rates. Everybody knows what that means. This was the type of place men took women for a few hours of pleasure, then dropped them off and drove home to the wife and kids.

If only I was that type of cheater, my life would be less complicated.

Emma isn't a woman I want to only sleep with. I want to be with her. I wish I'd never said "I do" to a woman like Karen. I wish I'd known someone like Emma existed. Everything in my world would have made sense if I had.

Instead, I made bad decision after bad decision when it came to women. That's the reason, after all, why I'm hiding Emma at this rundown place.

"What are we doing here, Owen?" Emma asks with a harsh tone.

I park the car and look at her innocently. "I thought maybe we could spend the night here. Talk things out."

She shakes her head. "I don't exactly want to spend a night here."

I can't believe her. She may keep a nice apartment but it's in the worst area in the city and she doesn't want to stay here? Why not? I think about telling her the truth but know that it's best to do it in a room.

"Okay," I say, not wanting to fight. "Let me just get a room and I'll be right back."

I get out of the car, looking around. I'm being

paranoid, I know it. There's no way for Alexandria to know where we are. Emma will be safe here, if I can get her to agree to stay.

There's no way of doing this without telling the truth, at least some of the truth.

I could lose Emma tonight. She's likely at the end of her rope with me already. She loves me though. She may not have said the words back to me this morning, but I know they're right on the tip of her tongue.

This is for her safety. She needs to understand that. Until I sort things with Alexandria, I need her to stay here.

I may not know what Alexandria plans to do, but I don't want to find out. As I speak to the motel clerk and pay for a one-night stay, I remind myself that this is a smart idea. Windsor may not be as big of a city as Toronto, but it's large enough to hide one person.

Alexandria won't know where she is. I'll have time to sort things.

The motel worker hands me the key and asks if I need anything else.

"If I need to extend the stay, is there availability?" I ask.

He blurts out a laugh. I immediately regret the question. Of course there is. I didn't see many cars in the lot and I'm sure this clerk isn't used to patrons staying longer than a few hours.

As I head back to the car for Emma, I stop in my tracks.

Emma may be safe here but what about Karen? What about Chloe? I pull out my phone and quickly text her.

"Hey, I'll be working late tonight. What are you guys up to?" I say.

I hope for a quick reply, but of course that doesn't happen.

Emma will be okay staying here, but what about my family? There are enough rooms to keep all of us safe here, but it likely isn't ideal to keep my family in the same motel as my mistress.

They could be in danger too though.

My phone buzzes, and thankfully, it's Karen. "At my dad's. Chloe may sleep over."

Relief washes over me immediately. Karen and Chloe are safe at my father-in-law's house. Chloe will be there all night too. Now I can focus on Emma.

I open the passenger side door for her, and Emma steps out. I gesture for her to follow me to our room. As soon as we're inside, she closes the door behind me and folds her arms.

"Time to talk, Owen," she says with a harsh tone. Usually, she has this glow about her, this aura of happiness, but the woman in front of me is anything but happy. She's pissed and rightfully so.

"It's not safe at your apartment right now," I say truthfully.

She shakes her head. "Who is she? A woman

followed me today and cornered me at the river, taking my picture. You know her. Don't lie to me, Owen. I know you do." She points a finger sternly at me.

I nod. "I do."

"Who is she? Your wife?"

I lower my head. "Not my wife. An ex. A crazy one. She works at the office with me. Her name is Alexandria."

Emma covers her face in disbelief. "I can't believe this. There's another woman."

"She's an ex, Emma! I saw her a few months before you. I ended things way before I ever met you."

She lets out a sigh. "You said that the woman 'wasn't your wife'." She uses air quotes. "So that means you're married as well."

I can't believe I let that slip out. With my concern over Emma, I wasn't paying attention to what I was saying. Emma did.

There's no way to lie around this. Perhaps it's better not to stretch the truth anymore.

"I am married," I admit. "But we're separated."

Emma's face drops as I say the words, and she covers her eyes, unable to look at me. "So you don't live with a terrible roommate?" Suddenly, she's realized another of my lies. "You never wanted me to go to your house, because your wife still lives with you. You're not separated, are you?"

I put my hands up in defence. "I am. We are. It's complicated. Separating isn't easy. Life is very complicated."

"Everything you told me was a lie," she says, her eyes wet. "Do I even know anything that's real about you?"

I lower my head. "You know I like my coffee black. You know I hate pickles. You know I love dipping fries in ice cream. You know my favorite movie is *The Godfather*, followed closely by *The Godfather Part Two*. I hate the third one. You know so much about me, Emma, and I know so much about you. I wasn't lying when I said I love you. I want to spend my life with you, Emma, if we can get over this. I know we can still can."

"Your wife sort of complicates things though," she says in disgust. "Your ex-girlfriend who's stalking me makes things even worse. Now I can't even go home because of you?" She shakes her head. "Why did you do this to me, Owen? I loved you."

Her words hit me in my chest. I feel like I'm out of my body when she says she loved me in the past tense. Our relationship is slipping from me and there's nothing I can do.

"I didn't expect someone like you to come into my life," I admit. "When you came to the open house the first day we met, I knew you were special. I couldn't tell you the truth. I couldn't tell you that I was still technically married. I couldn't say that. You would never have given me the time of day if I had. You would have instantly moved onto the next lucky man who would get to be with you. I lied. I lied! But it's because you were worth it."

I look at her, a tear of my own forming. I thought

my words could sway her, at least momentarily. They have no effect. She stares back at me, her arms still folded.

It's quiet in the motel room as we stare at each other. I wait for her to say the next words, hoping it's something that shows I still have a chance. Her face lightens and her arms go to her side. She takes a deep breath and steps closer to me. My heart beats faster, thinking she's going to kiss me.

Everything will be okay.

"It's over, Owen," she says. "I'm done with this." She turns from me and opens the motel door.

"Wait!" I call out. "Don't go. You need to stay here, please!"

She huffs. "I'm not staying here with you, Owen."

"It's not safe to go home, Emma," I say. My heart is broken, but I can't have her leave and put her safety at risk.

"I'm not afraid of Alexandria," she says, turning from me again.

"Emma, please, stay with me," I plead.

She looks at me with disgust. A face I never imagined she'd make at me. "I can't believe I fell for you. Your lies. I thought what we had was special."

"It is!" I shout. "Please, trust me when I say it is. I never had this with another woman."

She lowers her head, and when she looks back at me, for a moment I see the woman who I fell for. Her expression quickly changes to one of disgust again. "I don't want to see you ever again."

CHAPTER 33

Emma

A cheater. Another cheater. Another terrible man in the laundry list that I consider my love life.

I called a taxi and as the driver took me to my apartment, I went over how the worst day of my life was going. First, my boyfriend's crazy ex stalks me near my house. Then, my supposed boyfriend tells me he's married. He also shares that the woman stalking me is unstable and I'm not safe.

He wanted me to stay at the cruddy motel with him. He had the nerve to believe I'd want to be anywhere near him after what he did to me.

The lies. I can't get over it.

I knew that him being married was a possibility. If it was just a crazy ex-girlfriend, I could have gotten over it. I can handle women like Alexandria.

What I can't stand are cheaters and liars.

I feel so sad at the idea that I'm the other woman. He's married and he's destroyed his vows by being with me. Who is his wife? Whose marriage was I ruining by being with Owen? Julie joked about me following him to see who the other woman is.

I think of my mother. I understand completely how she became so unstable to the point of wanting to kill my dad after finding out he cheated on her. I hated him after I saw some strange woman kissing him that wasn't my mom.

I wish Mom never brought Julie and me to see what my father was doing. She did though.

We saw our dad kiss the other woman. We watched in horror as Mom went after our dad with a knife. It was Julie who called the police.

Afterwards, Dad left. Mom went to prison. Grandma and Grandpa tried to raise us the best they could, despite their age and low income.

Then Mom killed herself. Dad never came to her funeral. My life was forever traumatized.

I know firsthand what cheating can cause in a marriage, not only for the couple but the children. It impacted me forever. Made me the woman I am today. Any negative personality traits are all rooted in the trauma that cheating created.

And now it's happening with my relationship. Only this time it's different. Owen's married. I'm the other woman.

My stomach is in knots. I feel nauseous, and it's not just the taxi's rough driving. Usually, I'd be happy with a driver who gets me to a destination quickly. Right now, I want him to slow down for fear that I'll throw up everything I've eaten in the past twenty-four hours all over his cab.

Thankfully, we're getting closer to my apartment. All I want to do is curl up in a ball and cry myself to sleep. Wish that today never happened.

I think of Julie. I don't need a crystal ball to know what she'll say or think. How did I not see this? How did I let my relationship with Owen go on for so long while being so blind?

He made me happy. He did. When he told me about his roommate situation, at first I questioned it. As I got to know Owen more, and fell hard for him, my questions became less and less.

The driver turns down onto one of the main streets downtown. That's when I see him. Owen, smiling at me from the corner outside. I want to scream as we pass his bus stop ad. His stupid face looking at me with such confidence. I quickly read the words beside his head.

"Your dream life starts with me."

I cover my mouth, wanting to shout curse words or just shriek until I pass out. How could I be so dumb?

For the past few days, I've tried to talk myself off a ledge. I've tried to give Owen a chance to show he's not like the others. He's worse.

He's married and had another mistress.

But, of course, he said he's separated from his wife. How can I even trust those words? He's still living with her, he admitted.

Is that common? I'd assume when people are on the verge of divorce, they'd want to be further apart than in the guest bedroom across the hall.

The driver stops outside my apartment, and I thank him before leaving. As he drives off, and I'm on the dark road alone, paranoia hits me again.

Owen was worried about my safety. He pleaded with me to stay. What if what he said was true? What if this Alexandria he works with is someone to worry about?

I look around the empty road and put my hand in my purse, gripping the small pocketknife as I walk up to the front door. Inside my purse, I let go of the knife and quickly take out my keys, opening the door. Once inside, I hurry to my apartment, shutting the door behind me and locking it.

Fear is taking over me as I look around my dark apartment. I try to calm myself, knowing that I'm safe. Taking several deep breaths, I begin walking around my home, turning on a few lights to feel less anxious. When my apartment is less intimidating, I go into the washroom.

I'm about to relieve myself but I can't get over how cold it is in the small room. Is there a problem with the heater? The building is archaic but it's never this chilly.

The rest of my apartment seemed fine, but the bathroom has a breeze. I look at the window and notice it's slightly open. It may be less than an inch away from closed, but I know I wouldn't have left it open. I never unlock my windows. I'm too vigilant to leave it unlocked in this neighborhood.

It hits me. Someone may have entered my house. I run outside the room and grab my purse, rummaging through it for the pocketknife. I hold it tightly, raising it in my hand as I stare around my apartment.

Am I being paranoid? It's not like I check the windows often or anything. Perhaps it was Owen who opened it one of the nights he was over.

Maybe it's Alexandria.

In my paranoid state, I call out for her. "Are you here? Are you in my house? I'm calling the police!" I wait for a response, but there's nothing.

With my nerves keeping me on high alert, I start to look around my apartment, the blade in my hand pointing in every direction I can. I start with the bathroom, quickly tossing the curtains to one side and pointing the knife into the bathtub.

I think I've watched *Psycho* too many times.

I take my time moving to my bedroom. I open my closet door quickly, pointing the knife inside as if Alexandria is there. Only she's not. I feel silly as I look under my bed, knife ready as if to fight back the monsters I used to think lived under there when I was a child.

I should be calming down as I look through possible hiding spots, but somehow, I'm becoming more nervous as I look around my living room. Nobody is here, I think, attempting to soothe my nerves. That's when I look at the closet by the front door. My place isn't large, and it's the only space left for an adult to hide.

Taking a deep breath, I walk towards the closet door, the knife raised at my side. When I open it, my eyes widen as a broomstick falls towards me. I let out a shriek as it hits the floor.

Nothing.

No boogeyman under the bed. No crazy exes in my closet.

CHAPTER 34

Karen

It should have been over. Everything should have happened today.

Instead, somehow, my dear husband swooped in at the last moment and saved his girlfriend. Did he know I was there somehow?

I stood in that dark closet for nearly thirty minutes after they left. She'd finally come home, I was about to open the closet door to reveal myself to her and end her life, and then a buzzer went off. I could hear Owen and her talking, and suddenly she left.

I began coming up with another plan. I could wait until they returned. My plan was to kill her when she was alone though. Putting myself against two people would be very difficult.

Then there was also the problem with my alibi. I wasn't supposed to be out too long. Murder Emma and go straight to Dad's.

That was the plan, and it all went to hell when my husband somehow managed to save his mistress.

I'm back at home now. Chloe's asleep in her bedroom. I sit on our marriage bed, alone, hating who I am and what I've let happen to me.

When I came up with my plan for killing Emma, it was all I could think about. I liked it and thought my plan was simple. Kill my husband's mistress. Frame him for the murder. Laugh to myself every night as he spends the rest of his life in jail for a murder he didn't commit. And the world would think he's a serial killer.

Looking back at it now, I realize how stupid I was. Why did I have to make life so complicated?

I should kill him. Easy. Direct and to the point.

Since Chloe is asleep, I scribble my thoughts and ideas in my journal. All of them dark and ending with me killing my husband. I'm motivated and ready to do what I must. I've hidden a kitchen knife under my pillow for when he returns.

I know I've lost it. The words in my journal show how far I've gone. I should have left Chloe at my dad's house. Instead, I picked her up. My father said I looked off. I feel off. I'm like a zombie walking around in a daze. I barely feel in control of my body.

It's all his fault.

He thinks he'll sleep another night in our marriage bed after screwing his girlfriend? It will be his last night ever.

There's one problem with my plan. I have no clue where my dear husband is. I know who he's with though.

It's nearly ten at night and he hasn't returned from his "late showing" of one of his listings. How in his right mind does he think I'll believe him? When he comes back home, does he really think I'll believe a word he says?

That's why he's the one who needs to die tonight.

I wanted to come up with this intricate plan where I get off scot-free, kill the woman he's sleeping with and ruin my husband's life. Let him feel what it's like to be ruined by someone else.

It's not good enough. It's not permanent. It's stupid.

The only way to get back at him is to kill him. And, when he comes home, that's exactly what I'll do.

CHAPTER 35

Owen

My life is over. It's that simple. Everything I had, everything that truly mattered, is no longer mine.

Tomorrow, I'll have to go back to work. Answer for why I left so abruptly. Soon, I'll have to return home and answer to my wife.

I'd rather go through the grilling my boss will give me than put up with Karen.

How could I let things get this way? I thought I could talk my way out of this mess, but it's my own words that gave me away.

This was why I never wanted to tell the truth to begin with. It would have brought me to the same place I am now, only quicker.

Now, I have to go back to a family who don't want me. A life of misery. What's the point of it all?

That is if Karen will take me back.

It's been hours since Emma left, but I stayed at the motel room. I can't move. I feel paralyzed. The only thing

I managed to do was try and call Emma. She didn't answer my calls or texts.

I should have paid the hourly rate at the motel instead of the overnight price. I'm not sure what I can do.

I should have gone home hours ago. Now it's late and all the lies I told Karen won't hold up. I'll have to have another difficult conversation. One that I can't talk myself out of.

I'm not the only one ignoring calls and texts. My wife's been attempting to reach me. I've seen her messages and missed calls. I haven't responded. Instead, I sit on the motel bed and do nothing except wonder how I let my life come to this.

It's all her fault. If it wasn't for Alexandria, I could have found a way to stay with Emma. I could have separated from Karen. If only I could go back in time, I would have done so many things differently.

Number one would be staying far away from Alexandria. She ruined me.

I think of Emma and tears well in my eyes, stemming from a sadness deep inside me that knows I'll never find a woman like her ever again. My heart is truly broken. I'll never recover.

After the things I've done, maybe this is exactly what I deserve. I hold my cell and open a text message.

"I'm at the Sleepaway Motel. Room thirteen. I'll wait for you."

I toss my cell across the bed in frustration. I pound the mattress in rage, my fist clenched as I imagine what

I'll do when she comes.

It doesn't take long until there's a soft knock at my door. When I open it, Alexandria stares at me intensely. Those sultry eyes that I used to love now cause digust inside me.

If this is what I deserve, what karma should be in store for Alexandria for what she did?

I force her inside the room and close the door.

CHAPTER 36

Karen

I want him dead. I want him to die! I want to kill him.

I will kill him!

I read back the words in my diary, knowing I've lost my sanity. I know that I'll be caught, but there's no going back. I no longer feel in control, and I don't care.

If I had an ounce of respect for myself or my child, I'd call the police. Or drive to the nearest hospital to admit myself for murderous insanity.

My house is a complete mess. It looks like the police raided my house. I've broken dishes and smashed picture frames. I've tossed pillows and smashed the wall with a potato masher. Somehow, in my erratic breakdown, Chloe never woke up.

I'm thankful. What she would see is a shell of the mother she knew. I barely recognize anything I do anymore.

All I want is revenge. All I want is for the pain to

stop. For Owen to die.

It's the only justified outcome that feels right.

As I read my journal entries from tonight and the madness in my words, I realize there's no going back. I've lost it.

I should have had Chloe stay with my father. I can't trust myself around her. Not only am I a failed wife but a failed mother too. What have I become?

Suddenly, I hear the front door open. "Karen!" The shriek of his voice startles me. Owen shouts my name again. "Karen, what happened?"

His voice. I barely recognize it. He must have seen the mess I've made in the house.

"Chloe!" he shouts. "Oh no, please!"

When I come down the steps slowly, his eyes widen, and he stares at me. "Are you hurt?"

I shake my head. Not physically hurt at least. But I'm truly broken.

All I've wanted for the past few hours is for him to come home so that I can finish this. I wanted closure from our marriage in the most personal way I can think of.

Owen falls to his knees, covering his face. "I'm sorry!" he says. "I'm so sorry. This is all my fault!" He looks at me again, tears streaming down his cheek. "I made so many mistakes, Karen. All I want to do is fix them. I just want to fix the mistakes. I was dumb. I love you, Karen! Please. Oh, please, can you forgive me for what I've done?"

His words sink in. My mouth opens, unable to find

words. There was a time where this was all I wanted from him. An apology. For him to genuinely say how much he loves me. Now, he's on his knees in front of me, pleading for me to forgive him.

It's too late. I try to shake off my feelings for him. The knife is upstairs under the pillow.

He stands up, taking small steps towards me. "I've been untrue to you. It was a mistake. I've been a terrible husband, and you've done nothing but be the most amazing wife ever."

I look at him strangely, wondering if I'm hallucinating.

He thinks I'm perfect? If only he knew what I was planning and what I wanted to do to him, he wouldn't say such things.

"I can't forgive you," I say, lowering my head.

"Please," he says. "We made each other happy, and we can do that again for each other. We can have the type of love that people don't think exists. I'll change. I'll do whatever you want me to do. Counselling. Whatever. I'll do anything to keep my family together. I love you. I love Chloe."

As I stare at him and listen to his words, tears of my own fall freely from my eyes. He takes another step towards me, opening his arms and closing them around my upper back.

"I love you, Karen," he whispers. "Please."

I cry into his chest as he repeats his words softly in my ear.

"Mommy," a tired voice says. I turn and Chloe is looking around the messy room. Papers flung around, food from the fridge tossed to the floor. She can't hide her confusion. "What happened?"

Owen hurries up to her, swooping her off her feet, holding her tightly to his chest. "Everything is going to be okay, Chloe," he says to her. He looks at me. "Everything is going to be okay."

CHAPTER 37

Emma

I *drank* last night.

It was one of many mistakes on my part. I attempted to sleep early, wishing that when I closed my eyes and opened them again that I'd wake up someone else. Somewhere else.

Far, far away from a man like Owen.

I still can't believe everything that happened last night. I'm still processing it all.

Sleeping early didn't work. I woke up thinking about him. Thinking about what he said. Had I not caught him saying he had a wife, would he have even mentioned her? The face he had when I called him out on his lie was priceless. His expression was enough for me to know the answer.

He wouldn't have.

Still, I can't help but wonder how I fell so hard for him. Was it all a lie? Was there anything true in what we had?

I stretch on the couch, exhausted from the terrible night I had. Very little sleep occurred.

It's been months since I've been to an AA meeting, but after last night, I'm due for an immediate one. I can't keep hurting myself because of others.

How could Owen do this to me?

Never give up on love. The words of wisdom from my late mother. It feels like the only wisdom I can remember from her, and it's complete garbage. When it comes to a man like Owen, love is not worth it.

Last night was not worth it. Everything we shared was a terrible memory that will stick with me.

Tonight, there's a meeting at eight at a nearby church. There's a decent-sized group that attend, at least that's what I found when I first went there some time ago. I can stay in the background of the crowd without having to share much. Take in the words and try forgiving myself.

It's hard when all I want to do is make more mistakes. Hopeless. That's how I feel. Doomed to repeat the self-destructive cycle over and over.

Julie will have a field day when I tell her what happened. I'm going to spare her the entire story. The crazy ex-girlfriend is something I'll omit. The unlocked window and stalking I won't share either.

I won't tell her what happened last night.

I turn on the television, hoping to take my mind off everything. A daytime host is interviewing an FBI profiler who's taken an interest in the Canadian serial murderer, the Heartbreak Killer.

"So, what kind of a person do you believe the Heartbreak Killer is?" the host asks, shuffling in his seat and staring at his live audience as he waits for an answer.

The agent looks like a stereotypical FBI man. A short haircut with a pencil mustache. He grins before answering. "The Heartbreak Killer is most certainly a man. One who has so much anger towards those around him that he's mastered the ability to hide his true feelings. He's meticulous. Careful. He likely stalks his victims for weeks. He knows their routines better than his victims."

"Interesting," the host says. "There is a debate going on, especially amongst true crime fans online, as to whether the killer is a man, a woman or a team."

The profiler laughs. "Yes, well, I can tell you that unlike the online detectives, and even the other authorities involved, I'm one of the few who's examined all files pertaining to his murders that are available. The Canadian authorities and Windsor Police have been very welcoming to me looking at their investigative work. I'm thankful to them for allowing me access to their information. When taking a look at everything as a whole, I've created a profile as to what I believe is the most accurate description of what the Heartbreak Killer looks like and his behaviour." He smiles. "Would you and your audience like to know my conclusions?"

The host smiles as the crowd cheers on, waiting for a response.

"There you have it," the host says. "We're all ears. Please share. As an FBI profiler, a leading authority in America, an agent who's accurately described other recent murderers, share with us all your conclusions on the Heartbreak Killer."

He nods, looking at the camera, knowing he has everyone's attention, even my own.

"The Heartbreak Killer is a Caucasian man. Married. I feel this is another case similar to the BTK killings. The killer is a man you'd never suspect. A man who is possibly known in his community. Secretly, he's a narcissist. A person who's capable of lying continuously to blend in with society."

The host smiles. "Well, it's not like any of us know a married white man who's too into himself." The crowd laughs as the host looks directly at the camera. "Honey, if you're watching, I know that might sound like someone you know, but I didn't do it." He puts a hand over his chest. "I swear."

The crowd erupts with laughter and so does the profiler. "Well, you were my top suspect," he says, pointing a finger at him playfully.

The host waves him off and looks back at the camera. "We'll be right back, but stay tuned to learn how he came to his conclusions about the Heartbreak Killer." As the crowd claps, an image of the Crimestoppers' logo comes up on the screen. "And if any of you have any information that could lead to the Heartbreak Killer's arrest, call the number on the screen. Your information is always confidential, and a cash reward is on offer."

The Heartbreak Killer sounds like someone I know too, I think.

I look at the number and turn off the television, wondering what I should do with the rest of my life. Listening to more daytime television doesn't seem to be helping me. Going outside my house doesn't seem like such a great idea as well. I'm turned off from running by the river at the moment.

Walking into the bathroom, I stare at the window. It's still locked, just as I ensured it was. I know for a fact I didn't unlock it. I'm certain it wasn't Owen.

I run through what I learnt last night. If I had any sense, I'd leave Windsor immediately. I'd never think about Owen ever again.

Instead of making sensible decisions, I made the worst ones I could have made last night. Instead of forcing myself to sleep, I left my apartment. I may not have much money for gas, but I took my beat-up car and drove back to the motel.

Owen was still there. I knew because his car was still in the lot. I should have left. Going back home was a much better option for me. But I needed to know who Owen really is. I needed to understand who the man I love is.

Just because I hate what he did doesn't mean I can turn off the emotional switch I have inside me. I wish it was that easy to completely hate him for what he did. Instead, I found myself curious.

It was a mistake.

It was a mistake when I saw Owen leave the motel. It was another when I followed him, driving far enough behind him that he hopefully didn't notice. He parked his car outside a house.

Already making so many mistakes last night, I made another. I parked my car on the street, sneaking up to the house. As I got closer, Owen shouted a woman's name.

"Karen!" he shrieked.

My heart sank as I got closer, needing to take a look at the woman the man I love is married to. When I was near a side window, I peered inside, my anger and curiosity turning to confusion as I saw the woman he embraced.

It was a woman I've met. One who's been inside my house.

Karen.

What is happening?

CHAPTER 38

Owen

Chloe's bowling ball slowly makes contact with a single pin, knocking it over. She screams as if she's got a strike. "I did it!" she cries, her arms in the air triumphantly.

Karen hollers her support from her chair. Chloe turns to me, and we high-five. "Good job, kiddo. But you're not done, you get a second shot."

Her eyes light up as she hurries to a ball rack, attempting to pick a ball up herself. Scared that she'll drop it and mangle her toes, I quickly grab her hands and guide her to the ball return.

"After you throw your ball, it comes back here. Look," I say, pointing at the belt. A few moments later, her kid-sized ball comes back.

"There it is!" she says with too much excitement.

I run my fingers through her hair playfully. "See, I told you." A bowling attendant approaches us with a large, hooked stick. "Sorry it took so long, guys," he says, looking at Karen and me. "Do you still want the bumpers up?"

Karen nods. "Yes, please." He nods ands raises the guards in our lane.

"What's he doing, Daddy?" Chloe asks.

I smile. "Well, he's putting up the bumpers so that our balls won't go into the gutters all the time. More fun this way." When he's done, I nod at the ball in her hand. "I'll walk up with you, but this time, you need to throw it yourself, okay?"

Chloe agrees and reluctantly walks up to the lane, rolling it on the floor well behind the line. It immediately heads towards the gutter, but with the guards up, the ball bounces to the other side, and back to the other slowly, all the way until it hits the center pin, knocking over more than half.

Chloe's eyes light up at her newly unlocked skill level. "Daddy, I knocked so many! Look!"

"Good job, buddy!" I shout as we high-five again. This time I show a little too much enthusiasm myself, throwing in a couple of hip thrusts as a celebratory dance. Chloe attempts the same, and Karen smiles, shaking her head.

"Look what you're showing our daughter," she says playfully.

I smile at her and our eyes connect. I wonder if she's thinking what I am.

It's weird how quickly your life can change. Last night, I felt everything was coming to an end. Things with Emma were over. I broke down in front of Karen. To my surprise, she didn't fight with me. She didn't demand to know everything I've been up to.

Strangely, she hasn't asked a single question.

This morning, I woke up and she was staring at me. At first, I could feel her anger as she slipped her hand under her pillow. A tear ran down her face.

"Can you ever forgive me?" I whispered to her. She didn't answer. Instead, she removed her hand from under the pillow and caressed the side of my face, kissing me.

Karen knows I've cheated on her. She doesn't know to what extent though.

Last night, I decided that the life I had was not worth living. That part of me was over. Emma never truly loved me. Karen does. I feel so stupid for looking for what I needed outside of our marriage, when what I wanted was at home all along.

Karen and I became distant to each other and to each other's needs. We are different people, but despite that, we can still come together. Today is a testament to that.

After family time together, Chloe will spend the night at Grandpa's. Mommy and Daddy need some alone time. We have a lot to talk about.

Mostly, I want her to know how committed I am to make our marriage work. I need her to understand that the mistakes I've made won't ever happen again.

Chloe runs up to Karen and hugs her. "Mommy, I'm so good at bowling. Did you see?"

She smiles. "I did, honey. Good job!" When Karen turns her head, her grin widens. I walk up to her, kissing her softly, while grabbing Chloe and bringing her in between us, embracing both of them at once.

How stupid was I for looking for love outside of this family that I have?

I was close to blocking Emma's number today. I see on my phone that she's read my messages. I know I shouldn't, but I feel like I need closure from that part of my life. I just want to see how she'll respond before removing her from my contacts.

When I called into work and advised them I'd need another personal day this morning, Doug, was initially upset. I told him the truth. Things are not good at home and my family needs my attention. Doug Hinchers is a family man himself. Married for over three decades. He understood.

And, so far, I'm not worried about Alexandria. After our talk last night, she's backing off. It hurts me knowing the extent I had to take things to get her to do so, but I know I'll never hear from her again.

This morning, I felt like a new man. Ready to rejuvenate my life, my marriage and my family. I'm refocused on what matters in my life.

My family. My wife.

With Alexandria out of the way and Emma out of the picture, that's exactly what I'll do. A clean start.

I'm up next to bowl. I toss the heavy ball down the lane. It thumps on the ground. Near the end of the lane, it would have gone straight to the gutter had it not been for the bumpers. Instead, it bounces and goes straight to the middle, causing all the pins to fall immediately. The sound of the strike causes me to cheer. Chloe shouts even louder! She's absolutely mesmerized.

"Daddy, you knocked over all the pins! You're really good."

I laugh. "Well, I'm only good with the bumpers on."

Karen throws next, managing to only get a few pins. Chloe attempts to comfort her, telling her someday she'll be as good as Daddy.

We let Chloe bowl on her own as Karen and I sit on the chairs, watching her and every so often glancing at each other.

"I'm having fun," I say.

She gives a thin smile and nods. "Me too. I'm glad you stayed home today."

I take a deep breath. "I know we have a lot to talk about, but I want you to know how much I love you." I look at Chloe. "How much I love our family. What I did—"

She puts up her hand. "I don't want to know," she says. When she looks up at me, her eyes are wet and full of emotion. "I just need you to promise you'll never do anything like that again."

"Never," I say. "I promise. I need you to trust me. What can I do to prove it?"

Karen smiles. "We talked about a trip for our anniversary."

I grin. "Right. You want to go back to the resort we spent our honeymoon at. I love that idea." When we kiss, her lips tremble as she sits back.

"I love you too, Owen."

CHAPTER 39

Karen

We made love, twice!

It's late now, nearly midnight. Despite being completely satisfied, I stare at the back of my husband's head, wondering what he's dreaming. Is it the night we had, or her?

He's said a lot to me last night and today. Made a lot of big promises. Does he mean a word of it? How can I trust what he says?

Today was so much fun. I felt normal. Happy. Like a family again.

The crazed woman I was last night and days prior feels almost nonexistent, until I remind myself what he's done to me.

Having one day with him made me feel so alive. Made me whole again. I loved watching him with Chloe at the bowling alley. It's hard for me to comprehend that this was the same man who was unfaithful to me, who hurt me.

A man I want to kill.

I slide my hand under my pillow, gripping the knife that I hid between the headboard and mattress. I take it out slowly, almost like the pillow is a sheath. When it's out, I stare at the blade, the dim light from the moon outside the open curtains shimmering as I tilt it.

And then I stare at my husband. It's time for me to put this where it belongs.

I take a deep breath when Owen starts to yawn and turn to me. I quickly hide the knife behind my back as he smiles at me and rubs his eyes.

"Hey," he says. "You okay?"

I nod and grin. "Just having trouble sleeping. It's been a rough week."

He takes a deep breath and agrees. "It has." He looks outside the window. "Did we forget to close the curtains?"

I laugh. "Both times, yes." I look out the window and into the dark house of my neighbors, the Bahers. For a change, they may have been the ones getting a show. I tighten my grip on the knife in my hand, ensuring that he doesn't see it. "I need to tell you something."

He yawns again. "What is it?"

I tap the knife against my back to try and find the words. "I really love you."

He grins. "I love you too." He leans in and kisses me softly, placing his hand on my lower back. My eyes widen as he inches closer to the blade.

I lean back from him. "Just need to go to the bathroom. I'll be back."

He nods. "Don't take too long." He smiles.

I take in his sultry stare as I leave, making sure to move the knife to my front as I turn from him. Hopefully, he didn't notice what was in my hand. He doesn't say a word as I leave the dark room.

I'm surprised by the one-eighty change in not only Owen but myself as well. Last night, I had murderous actions planned for when I saw him, but when he came home, sobbing, pleading with me, I gave in. Then Chloe came into the room, and my heart melted more.

My dark thoughts escaped me for more positive ones. What if he means what he says?

What if he wants to start over with me? He admitted to his mistake and said it won't happen again.

It may be naive for me to believe him, but he's my husband. The father of my child. The cynic in me wanted to take the knife out from behind my pillow and end our marriage. I didn't go through with it, because part of me knows that he can change.

People can change. My father is the perfect example.

I hated him. I hated how he treated my mother. After she died, he completely turned his life around. He changed. Now, he's easy to be around. I enjoy spending time with my dad, which is something I never thought would be possible.

I walk past the bathroom, tapping the knife along the side of my jogging pants. As I make my way to the kitchen, I take one last look at the knife, wondering how I could have ever thought of using this on Owen.

I was truly insane last night. Within twenty-four hours, my entire mood shifted. My family is whole again.

I'm happy.

I slide the knife back in the knife block. I know Owen is waiting for me in the bedroom, but I need to make sure how I'm feeling at this moment is noted. Any time I feel upset or angry with Owen in the future, I can take a look back at my own words to realize there's hope.

When I enter my office, I open my leatherbound journal to the next blank page. Before I write how I'm feeling, I decide to go through a few entries, sitting and examining my own dark thoughts, terrified at not only what I wrote but what I actually did.

I waited in Emma's apartment. If it wasn't for Owen, I know I would have killed her. In the state of mind I was in, I was capable of anything. Not only planning her murder, but something much more sinister. Murder and framing my husband for it.

In my darkest moments, I was going to make my husband the Heartbreak Killer. Emma was going to be the serial killer's latest victim.

Of course, my husband is not a murderer. I'm not one either. Perhaps my plan was doomed from the start. Could I really get away with framing my husband for a murder? Not just any murder but setting him up to be the

Heartbreak Killer?

The idea was stupid, beyond belief. I read my own words in my journal, one that ironically Owen bought for me to plan the end of his life.

When my plan to murder Emma failed, I went to the next best option in my mind. Killing Owen. Had he come home earlier, I would have gone through with it. I didn't care at that time. Thankfully, he didn't come home until late in the evening.

I was much more tired by then and my murderous thoughts waned as the night got darker. The flame was reignited briefly when I saw him but was quickly put out when he broke down in front of me.

Today is a new day. The terrible things I did yesterday was someone else. The nightmare Owen put me through is over.

I don't want him to tell me what he did behind my back. I already know the truth. He didn't ask me what happened to the house, why it was destroyed, but he did help me clean it up, and that's what I focus on.

It felt symbolic, us cleaning the house together. Because of his lies and unfaithfulness, I destroyed the house and would have destroyed him, but now it's clean.

He won't tell me what he did, and I won't tell him what I planned. Seems fair enough to me.

This is a new day for us and for our marriage.

I take a pen from my desk drawer and write on a blank page. It's only a few words but with it being late and Owen expecting me in the bedroom soon, I write enough to remind myself of how grateful and loved I feel tonight.

"Everything will be okay now."

CHAPTER 40

Emma

A normal woman would not put herself through what I'm doing. They would leave. Be upset and look for comfort, cry a bunch, and move on. I'm not like that though. I wish I was.

I imagine my sister watching me right now, her head shaking, with a disappointed stare. She's right to feel that way. I'm disappointed in myself.

I didn't go to my AA meeting today. I should have. It ended hours ago. Thankfully, I didn't resort to my old ways, but it's so tempting.

No, instead of putting myself back on a solid path in life, I'm stalking my boyfriend and his wife. I let my own thoughts sting me as I sit outside Owen's house.

I witnessed a lot today. I wish I never saw any of it. I stepped up to their windows, watching them talk in the living room. I saw them go upstairs to their bedroom. I heard the faint sounds of ecstasy as they rekindled their marriage.

I stayed in their backyard, covering my face. I've

been here since, trying to convince myself that what I'm doing is beyond stupid.

I should just leave.

I can't though. It's not enough to just have curiosity about the truth Owen's been hiding from. When I followed him from the motel back to his house, I knew it was dumb to do. He told me he was married. I knew that, and despite that knowledge, I needed to see it for myself.

I wanted to see her. I can't be mad at a married woman for their husband sneaking behind their back. I reminded myself I was the other woman in this situation.

Knowing all of this, I still decided to follow him back to his real house. But when I saw his wife, everything changed.

I wanted to know what she'd look like. Was she pretty? The cold side of me hoped I was prettier than her. Once I discovered the truth, I'd rather his wife was a supermodel.

Karen.

The woman who was outside my house, crying. The woman who came back and knocked on my door, who I invited inside for tea. The same woman who I talked openly about Owen with. She's his wife?

I sit outside Owen's house as I remember the things I said to Karen in my house. I had my boyfriend's wife over for tea.

I can't get over that.

I also can't get over what else I've concluded.

Obviously, Karen crying outside my door was not coincidental. She must have discovered where I lived somehow.

Not only was my boyfriend's wife stalking me, but so was his ex-girlfriend. His previous mistress before me. The idea of it all enrages me to the point where I curse out loud in the darkness.

I look around the backyard and the side of Owen's house, where I'm hiding. No one is outside, and nobody is awake inside.

So, why am I still here?

It's because I can't shake the feeling that more is going on with the love square between Owen, his wife, his ex-girlfriend and myself.

I discovered my bathroom window was unlocked last night. It took a lot of processing to figure out who did that. Out of the four of us, only three were in my bathroom. I obviously didn't unlock it. Owen wouldn't have.

That leaves Karen. But why would she do that? I need to know.

I take a deep breath. I should just leave. Why am I doing this? Owen isn't worth this. My sanity isn't worth this either. All it does is make me want to make bad decisions. AA is a much better decision, and yet I can't move.

A light comes on inside Owen's kitchen. I can't help myself as I look inside and see Karen inside. She moves to another room on the other side of the house. I quickly go around the house and see her inside an office, writing something in a leatherbound journal.

She turns off the light and heads out of the room. I can hear her stomp up the stairs, no doubt heading back to the bedroom she shares with Owen. My heart sinks at the idea.

I stare into the dark room and the journal on the desk.

CHAPTER 41

Karen

It's been a week since Owen and I made up and I'm still on cloud nine. Not just with my marriage but life in general. When everything is fine in your life, it's easy to have such a positive outlook.

Owen is staying true to his word. I thought the devotion he showed since coming clean to me would have waned, but it's even stronger. We've had more family days with Chloe, going out to Red Lobster for their all you can eat shrimp night. It's one of our favourite places to dine, but we haven't been in over a year. My dad is watching Chloe overnight.

Tonight is another date night for Owen and me. I can't wait. This morning, before leaving for work, he kissed me so passionately that when Chloe walked in and witnessed us, she giggled hysterically. All I can think about are his lips on mine. I can't wait for his body to be mine as well.

It's like we're having a renaissance period in our marriage. We're rediscovering how to pleasure each other, and it's been incredible. The way he takes me in his arms so tightly while we kiss and make love is all I can think about.

And tonight, he's all mine.

It's not just the sex though. Emotionally, he's all mine too. We're talking like we used to when we first started dating, when we were infatuated with each other. He has an interest in knowing me again and it feels like there's so much we both missed out on during the dark period of our marriage.

I've already dropped Chloe off at my dad's house. He told me to not worry about picking her up early tomorrow. Chloe and he made plans to go to a few different playgrounds around the city. There's one that's in the shape of a pirate ship downtown by the river. It's all Chloe talked about before I dropped her off.

"Grandpa's taking me to the pirate ship park!" she'd yell, followed by her grunting like a pirate.

For once, everything in my life is perfect.

A knock on my front door changes everything. I hurry across my living room as the person outside knocks louder. When I open it, a woman stares back at me.

"Are you Mrs. Pearson?" she asks. She's wearing dark blue jeans with a grey blazer. What immediately catches my attention is the gold shield hanging around her neck.

"Yes, that's me," I say cautiously. I think of Chloe and my father. Now there's a cop at my door. Immediately, I jump to the worst case scenario. "Is everything okay? My daughter?"

She puts a hand up to relieve me. "I'm here just to talk to you, actually. My name is Detective Jennifer Nahas." She puts her hand in her pocket and gives me her card. I read her name and her position below it. Homicide Detective. My eyes widen.

"What's this about?" I say, worried about what will come out of her mouth. Did someone witness me breaking into Emma's house? Do the police somehow know what I was planning to do?

"Can we speak inside?" she asks with a small grin.

I reluctantly nod and gesture for her to come into my living room. She sits in a love seat, facing me. I offer her drinks, but she declines.

"Do you know much about the people who work with your husband?" she asks.

I take a deep breath, trying to calm myself and focus on answering her question, which thankfully is not about me. "Not well," I admit. "He doesn't really spend time with them outside of work."

She nods. "What about Alexandria Sutton? Do you know her?"

I look at her strangely. "Yes," I say. "She's the receptionist at my husband's real estate company. Is something wrong?"

The officer examines my face as she answers. "Her parents are quite concerned about her safety. She's been missing for over a week. She has not been to work all week. Her employer is equally concerned as absences are not typical for her."

I look down at the card in my hand. "Do you think something terrible happened to her?" I ask.

"That's what I'm looking into, Mrs. Pearson." She shuffles in her chair. "When was the last time you spoke with Ms. Sutton?"

Why is a homicide detective in my house asking about Alexandria? I try my best not to start demanding she tell me and instead answer more of her questions. "I believe it was at a Christmas party in December. I went to my husband's office party."

"And you haven't spoken to her since?" she asks.

I shake my head. "No," I say, clearing my throat. "Why are you here at my house today? Why are you asking me these questions?"

The detective looks at me empathetically. "Are you aware of any friendship that your husband may have had with Ms. Sutton outside of work?"

I look at her strangely. "No," I say. "What's happening here? Are you saying that my husband and Alexandria were sleeping together?"

The officer takes a deep breath. "We have confirmation from her parents that she and your husband may have had some type of relationship for some time."

I let out a laugh in my moment of confusion. "What? Alexandria?" I say, confused. I wanted to blurt out that my husband was cheating on me, but it was with another woman. Or so I thought.

How many women has my husband cheated on me with? I feel lightheaded as I sit across the living room from the detective.

"Do you know where your husband was last Thursday?" the detective asks.

I shake my head but don't answer. My head is still processing the detective's words. Owen had an affair with Alexandria. Now she's missing. The detective asks me the same question again.

"No," I say this time. "He was out of the house. He said he had a late showing for a house listing." I don't tell her the full truth, only Owen's version of it. I don't talk about Emma. I don't talk about my own actions that night. The officer isn't here for me.

"Do you know what time he came home that night?" she asks.

I shake my head again. This time I'm telling the full truth. It was late, but I was a little out of it that night with my own issues.

I look at the detective, our eyes locked on each other. I can see the empathy in her gaze. She must sense that I never knew about Alexandria.

"Are you telling me you think my husband killed Alexandria Sutton?" I ask.

She looks at me a moment before answering. "We may need you to come to the police station."

CHAPTER 42

Emma

What I'm doing creeps myself out. It feels odd. Despite how it makes me feel, I continue to sit on the park bench, watching them.

A little girl named Chloe plays with her grandfather at a playground. I've been watching them interact with each other for some time, thinking about everything.

Owen has a daughter, which was another thing my boyfriend failed to mention. With each new revelation I have about Owen, the more I despise him.

How did I fall for his lies so easily? It's as if he knew how vulnerable I was, how much I wanted to find someone like who he pretended to be, that he knew what to say and how to act. I fell head over heels for a body of lies, not an actual person.

And now I'm watching his child as she's being pushed by her grandpa. She giggles as he makes sounds like a pirate.

"Where's my buried treasure?" he shouts.

"I don't know, Grandpa," she says honestly. She gets off the swing and demands for him to chase her up the playground that's in the shape of a pirate ship.

He laughs. "I'm too old to chase you," he says. "Go find my buried treasure." He waves at her, but she looks confused.

"I don't have a shovel," she says with a confused look.

He shakes his head. "Just go have fun." He laughs. She understands now and runs up the ship, making her way to a long slide, blending in with the other children who are screaming and running around.

The grandpa makes aching sounds as he sits on a bench near mine. "I can't keep up with her," he jokes. It takes me a moment to realize he's speaking to me.

I laugh nervously. "Yeah, well, it's not easy."

"How many do you have?" he asks, putting his leg over his knee with a faint smile. When I don't answer immediately, he rephrases it. "How many children?"

"Oh," I say, looking around the busy playground. "Two."

"Girls or boys?" he asks. "That's my grandchild, Chloe. She's four."

I nod. "Two girls," I say with a thin smile. "Julie and Emma." I look around the playground. "I don't even know where they are. I suppose I should be anxious."

He laughs and waves me off. "It's always complete chaos when I bring Chloe here." As if she heard her name,

Chloe runs up to her grandpa.

"Can we buy a toy?" she asks. "Please!"

He shakes his head. "You can't get a toy every time I see you," he says.

"But I really want this Barbie doll," she says. "She has this unicorn sweater on. And," she says louder, "she has a horn on her head! Please! I've been so good."

He laughs. "Well, you're always good. Maybe Santa will give it to you."

"Santa!" she says, unable to hide her tone of disappointment. "That's going to take forever."

He laughs again. "Just go play, dear. We'll go back to my place and have ice cream."

"Yay!" Chloe shouts enthusiastically as she runs back to the playground, joining the growing number of children.

I take a moment to search for Chloe in the sea of children's faces. Kids are so innocent. If only they knew how terrible their parents are. I never understood how bad my own mom and dad were until much later in life. I stand up from the bench.

"Have a good day," I say to the old man as he smiles and nods.

"You as well."

As I walk away, all I can think about is how many lies Owen told me. I think about everything I've discovered about him. I think about everything I've learnt about his wife.

It hits me that I've managed to forget to bring my fake children with me as I leave the playground. I look back where Chloe is speaking with her grandpa again, pulling at his arm until he reluctantly gets up and starts to chase her around some trees. She's shouting with laughter as he gets closer.

I let that image of my boyfriend's daughter stay with me all the way until I'm back at my own apartment.

Cheaters.

Mom said she'd never give up on love. She should have. Cheaters don't love anything except themselves.

There's another AA meeting tonight, and I know I won't go. What I'm doing is so self-destructive, but it doesn't seem to faze me.

In my despair, I call the one person who has my back. She picks up the phone immediately.

"Hey," Julie says. "I was wondering when you were going to call me back. I've been trying to reach you. I was so nervous when you didn't text or call back. Is everything okay?"

It was mean not to call her. She phoned many times and an even larger number of texts, yet I've avoided her like the plague for the past week. The only thing I managed to do, just to assure her I wasn't dead, was when she asked if I was okay, I replied with a thumbs up.

"I'm sorry," I say. I take a moment to find the words. "He's married. He has a child."

"Oh," she says in a somber tone. There's silence

between us for what feels like forever. "I'm so sorry, Emma. Screw him. What can I do?"

My sister, always a pragmatist. She doesn't like it when I vent to her. She just wants to move on to how to solve the problem I have. That's partly why I waited to call. I wasn't ready for problem solving. I just wanted to sulk.

Sulk and stalk my ex-boyfriend.

I sit on the couch and cover my face as I say the words. "It hasn't been well for me out here," I say. I take a deep breath before I ask. "Do you think I could come back? To your place?"

There's a pause on the other end, and for a moment, my heart sinks as I worry she'll say no.

"Of course, Emma," she says. "I'm always here for you. When do you want to come?"

"Soon," I say.

I should just go now, but I can't. After what I discovered about Owen and Karen, I need to stay a little longer.

As I end my call with my sister, I make yet another mistake. With my cell still in my hand, I text him.

"Owen, we need to talk."

CHAPTER 43

Owen

Another house sale is completed. The new homeowners are happy. It's the part of this job that I love the most, telling my clients that they sold or bought their new home.

Today was double the joy. A couple called about a listing I had and wanted to see the house. No problem. It's a single-family house. Low square footage and only two bedrooms. The perfect starter home.

Perfect for the couple that I met today. A young man and a very pregnant wife. Instantly, they told me their motivation was to move into a new house before the baby came, which could have been during the showing judging from her belly.

They liked the pictures online and tried their best to hide how much they loved the house. The two would talk secretly amongst themselves as I sat in the kitchen and went through my emails on my phone.

The house was decently priced for the market. The seller was motivated to sell because of a recent divorce.

The young couple came into the kitchen, both smiling and wanting to make an offer.

I always found that part of my job so ironic. While one couple breaks up and moves out, another new couple moves in with hopes and dreams ahead of them, not knowing that the former residents' shattered dreams are left inside these four walls.

Better yet, they didn't come in with a realtor of their own. Full commission for the house. As I drove back to the office to bring in the paperwork for the sale, I was elated with myself.

I worried what the breakup with Emma would do to me. I truly loved her. But she left, and somehow, I found my way back to my wife. Back to my family. I wonder how I could have ever drifted away so far from them to begin with.

I've had two sales this week alone. Most realtors would be happy making one sale every few months.

I park outside my company's building, grabbing the folders and paperwork, when my cell goes off. I remind myself that I need to take the listing off the market now that I've got the sale and everything is finalized. I hope it's this couple I met last week about listing their house in South Windsor. Beautiful house and it will sell fast. With my track record growing, Doug Hinchers will be happy to throw more work my way. I feel I'll have a strong last two sales quarters this year.

As I look at my cell, I realize I'm not that lucky.

"Owen, we need to talk," Emma's message reads. I lower my head.

I must have texted and called her several dozen times with no response whatsoever. After a while, I assumed she blocked me. Hell, I even drove past her apartment to see if she still lived there. She had talked about living with her sister who lived out in the country somewhere.

I thought she'd left the city until I spotted her leaving her building one day. I left immediately, hoping she didn't see me.

All I wanted was for her to respond, and now she has. In my mind, I thought it would be an angry response with all caps and exclamation marks. Her telling me what a piece of crap I am.

No, that's not the case. She wants to talk.

I know from my sales career that this is more than likely positive. A client doesn't call you back if they're not interested. An ex doesn't text you if she wants nothing to do with you.

This was what I wanted, so why do I feel so terrible? The answer is obvious. I just made up with Karen. Things are better than they've been in a long time. I feel connected to my wife again.

I can't deny though that I still have feelings for Emma. And she wants to talk. Shouldn't I at least see what she has to say?

I slip my phone into my pocket, trying to get her message and thoughts of her out of my head. I shouldn't. I know I shouldn't.

I think of her smile. Her lips. Her body. My soul

aches wanting just to be near her again. I never thought I would get a chance after what happened at the motel.

Leaving my car, I try to change my mindset. I don't need to respond immediately. She took over a week to respond to me. She can wait now.

When I enter the building, I smile at the receptionist. A young woman who's replaced Alexandria all week.

"Morning, Mr. Pearson," she says with a welcoming smile.

"Hey, Sarah," I say, walking by.

She's gorgeous. Only twenty-five. A petite brunette who wants to be a social worker and is taking night school to get her dream job. She tells me how her night school is going. I let her know I have to go but will circle back later to hear how she did on her essay she got back from her professor last night. From the look on her face, it wasn't a good grade.

As I get closer to my desk, Doug Hinchers approaches me. "Owen," he says with a serious tone.

"Hey, Doug," I say. "Good news. I sold that house in Forest Glade. It's—"

"The police are here," he interrupts.

"What?" I say, surprised.

He nods towards the meeting room. "She's waiting to speak to you."

"What's this about?" I ask.

He gives me a stern look. "I'm hoping you can

tell me afterwards. Before you came, I was asked some questions that were very confusing. We need to talk after."

"About what?" I say.

He looks away. "After speaking with the detective, come to my office." Without waiting for my response, he leaves.

I stare at the meeting room. Its door is open. Before I go, I drop off my folders of paperwork. I notice a few colleagues gawking at me as I pretend to act normal.

Looking at the meeting room again, I reluctantly head towards it, peeking my head inside. A woman with a grey blazer greets me with a thin smile.

"You must be Owen Pearson," she says. "Please, close the door behind you."

CHAPTER 44

Karen

I sit in the kitchen, waiting anxiously for my husband to return. My heart drops when eventually I hear keys at the front door.

"Karen?" he calls out.

"Kitchen," I say with a harsh tone.

"Where's Chloe?" he asks as I hear him in the living room, taking off his dress shoes. I see him moving around the living room and tossing his suit jacket on the couch. I see the edge of his cellphone in the pocket.

"Dad's," I say, continuing with my one-word answers.

"Good," he says after a moment. "Listen, we may need to have a raincheck on our date night." He comes into the kitchen with a small grin. "Something came up at work. I have to head back out soon. Shouldn't take too long," he says confidently.

I'm still in awe of his ability to blatantly lie to me.

"Alexandria," I say, giving another one-word

answer, but this time, I have his complete attention. His mouth opens as he stares at me. I think it's obvious from his reaction how angry I look. "You were screwing her too!" I pound on the wood table. I'm surprised that it startles him enough to take a step back.

"Karen," he pleads. "Listen, I—"

"You were screwing your receptionist at your office!" I yell. "Who else? How many more whores did you put your dick into?" When he stares at me in response, I pound the table again and stand up, pointing a finger at him. "I believed you when you said you loved me!"

"Karen, I do," he says softly. "I made mistakes. I wanted to tell you, but you said you didn't want to know."

I cover my face. "I thought it was Emma! I didn't know you had a list going. I didn't realize my husband was screwing everyone except his wife!"

Suddenly, his worried expression changes to confused. "How do you know her name? Emma. I never told you about her."

I shake my head. "You think you're so suave, telling me all the lies. I could see right through you! I can see through you now." I think of the receptionist. "And now the police are knocking at my door. A detective told me about your affair." I lower my face. "They think you killed her. She's missing."

"I know," he says. "A detective came to my office today."

"Detectives Nahas," I say. He nods. "What did you say?"

He takes a deep breath. "Nothing. She asked questions, but I said I wasn't willing to talk without a lawyer. I was told to get one and have them call her office immediately."

I look at him, amazed. "I didn't think you had that inside you. Killing a woman?"

"I didn't!" he shouts back.

"No, you just screwed her," I say mockingly. "How can I trust that you're telling the truth now?"

"This is ridiculous, Karen," he says, waving his hand at me. "I wanted to mend our marriage but it's obvious there's nothing left to repair. It's too broken."

"What does that mean?" I yell.

He takes a step closer to me, a finger of his own pointing at me. "I want a divorce. It's over!"

I shake my head. "I should talk to the police. I'm sure I can help them with their investigation into you."

"I'm leaving," he says.

"Where to?" I ask. "Back to your girlfriend, Emma? Or do you have another woman in line to replace her already?" He doesn't respond and turns to leave.

I beat him to it and brush past him into the living room. On the couch, in his navy suit jacket, is his cell. My husband hates keeping it in his pants pocket after he read some article about lower sperm counts and cellphone emissions.

I grab his cell phone and wave it at him. "I'm sure the police would love to see what messages you have on here, wouldn't they?"

"Give me back my phone, Karen!" he shouts, trying to intimidate me with his size and booming voice. It won't work. The kitchen knife I've hidden in the back of my pants dares him to test me. He steps towards me as I step backwards.

He takes another step, and I quickly run into the bathroom, locking the door behind me. He pounds on the other side, demanding I open the door and give him back his cell.

I ignore him as I attempt to unlock his phone. There's a fingerprint required but he also has a swipe password. I make a few zigzags on the screen with my finger, attempting to open it but failing.

My husband isn't one to change things though. It's hard to concentrate with him yelling and threatening to break in the door, but I remember his password from an old phone he had years ago. I make a Z formation with my finger and bring my finger up. I can't help but smile when it opens to the main screen. I immediately open his texts.

My heart sinks when I see the first message from her. He even labeled her contact as Emma. The man doesn't even have enough respect to hide his mistress in his contacts.

I open the last message and read it out loud, cringing as the words hit me.

"Emma: Owen, we need to talk!" I shout.

He bangs on the door louder. "Karen, put my phone down right now! I swear!"

"You: Where do you want to meet?" I say, reading his response. He's talking to her still. I should have never believed a word Owen said to me. I read the last message from Emma. "The same place as last time. The same room." I shake my head in disbelief. "You're going to meet her right now?" I shout. "I can't believe you!"

"Open this door now!" he demands. I can feel his foot smashing into the other side. The door makes a cracking sound. The vibration from the kick hurts, and I take a step back.

"Let's see your messages to poor missing Alexandria," I say. "I'm sure you've been talking to her lately also, knowing you."

"Karen!" he yells loudly. He boots the door viciously, breaking in the cheap material to the point where there's a small opening. Another few kicks and it flies open, barely hanging on the hinge.

He steps inside quickly, cornering me. Without hesitation, I reveal the large knife I've been hiding and point it towards him. My attempt to protect myself is useless as he grabs my forearm and takes the knife from me, throwing it behind him. He pushes me against the wall and easily pries his phone out of my fingers.

"I hate you, Owen!" I shout in his face. He gets closer to me and lets go of my body. He turns and walks away, towards the front door, not slowing as I continue to scream. "I hate you, Owen! I hate you!"

CHAPTER 45

Emma

It's late when I park near the Sleepaway Motel. The neon sign above the lot blinks, casting a sickly, erratic glow on the cracked pavement.

The only vehicles parked here are one near the front desk lobby, who I expect is the person working late, and Owen's by our room further down.

Good. He's here. Time to get this over with. I've practiced and rehearsed what I want to say to him many times. I felt like I was back in high school, auditioning for a part in the school play. I literally sat in my apartment, practicing my lines and even at times pretending to respond as I thought Owen might.

I need closure from our relationship.

No more hiding outside his house or following his wife and child. I hated myself watching his daughter play with her grandpa.

If I finish in time, there's an AA meeting in a few hours. I've already packed up my apartment. My gas tank is full, and I'm nearly ready to leave this city forever.

All that's left is Owen. I can't leave without telling him how I truly feel.

I knock on the door softly, and moments later, Owen opens it with a faint smile.

"I was worried you weren't going to come tonight," he says.

"I needed to see you," I say. "Can I come in?"

He nods and opens the door fully, then closes the door behind me, turning to me. "I want you to know, before we talk, that I broke things off completely with my wife. It's over." He lets out a nervous laugh. "It's kind of good that I'm here tonight. I think I'm sort of homeless at the moment."

I don't smile or laugh at his pathetic joke. It's likely a lie anyways, and even if it's not, I don't care. I get straight to the point, just as I practiced.

"You have a child," I say, shaking my head. He doesn't respond. "I can't believe you have a child and a wife."

"Emma—"

I cut him off. I'm not interested in more lies. "I never told you about my past. About my dad. I told you a little about my mom. You know she died." I shake my head in disgust. "I didn't tell you why she killed herself though. My mom almost killed my dad because he cheated on her. After she went to jail, she killed herself. I never saw my dad again after she almost murdered him."

"I should have told you," he admits.

I don't care about his ploys to get me to sympathize with him. I have no emotional availability to give a shit about how he's feeling.

"You should have never got with me to begin with," I shout, reminding myself to keep my voice down.

He nods and gives me a smug look. "I thought you wanted to talk, Emma. Is this what you really want to do? Rail into me with how terrible I am? No thanks. I'd rather not. How about you just leave!"

I shake my head. "No, I'm not here just to tell you how much of a piece of shit you are, Owen. I know what you did. I saw Alexandria that night."

"What?" he says, surprised. "What are you on about now?"

"I came back to this motel. I saw what you did to her." I take a deep breath, reminding myself how she looked the last night she was alive. "You beat her. Her eyes were black and blue when she left the motel room. I know what you did. You're not just a shitty husband, a shitty dad, not just a liar and philanderer. You're a woman-beater too."

I stare at him blankly, enjoying how much fun I'm having ripping into this pathetic man I used to love.

He looks at me for a moment. I wait for his fiery response. Instead, he smirks and turns to the motel door, locking the dead bolt. He shakes his head and looks at me. "Why is it that every woman in my life is driving me absolutely insane?"

CHAPTER 46

Karen

My husband thinks so little of me. He doesn't think I can figure out where he's going. At first, I was worried I wouldn't be able to.

I drove by Emma's apartment first. Nobody was home. I attempted to get inside her place through the window that I unlocked, but it's since been secured. I looked through every window I could for any sign of life.

Nobody was there. Not Emma or my husband. Although I did notice something strange. No personal items were in her house. Everything looked very tidy inside. A box was near the window with newspapers inside.

I screamed outside her apartment window, not caring who heard my shrieks of frustration. After Owen put his hands on me, confirming that he was going to see his girlfriend, all I could think about was sticking my knife inside him.

Emma too.

In fact, I brought a knife for each of them. Tonight,

there is absolutely no going back. No matter how much he pretends to sob and tell me how much he loves me. No matter how much she cries to spare her worthless life. Tonight, they'll both die.

I don't care anymore. I don't care about framing anybody for murder or being free from suspicion. In fact, I may not be alive myself much longer. I don't care anymore.

All that matters is that Owen and his dear Emma join me.

There was only one problem with my plan. I had no clue where they were. That was until I was able to rationalize where they could possibly have gone to meet.

If not her apartment, it must be somewhere else. The text I read said it was a room. Somewhere in the city, my husband and his floozy are sharing a hotel room, not knowing their time together is about to come to an end.

I called my credit card company. Owen and I share an account. This wasn't the first time they spent a night somewhere else besides Emma's apartment. If Owen was stupid enough to use his own credit card, I'd find him.

I let out a laugh at how pathetic he is when the customer service representative gave me the motel's name. The Sleepaway Motel.

I'm in the parking lot now, horrified at my husband's taste in where he takes his mistress for a good time. The type of place that rents beds by the hour. It's disgusting, but I suppose Emma isn't picky, seeing how she lives.

I see his car alone in the parking lot. There are a few rooms near where he's parked, but only one has a light on inside. I get out of my car and stroll up to the door.

I have no plans about how to proceed. No logic about what I'm about to do. I've lost my ability to think straight on my way here. I don't even have a journal to write out what I'll do. Somehow, I misplaced it in my fit of rage. I'm acting purely on instinct. I'm following my murderous thoughts to their natural conclusion.

The door to the motel room is slightly open. Even better. My lucky night. I worried how I'd get inside. Now the question is, how can I cause the most damage?

Owen's strong. He took the knife out of my hand at the house easily. Emma won't be so capable. I'll enjoy killing her first and watching my dear husband realize the woman he loves is dying as I attack him. With the element of surprise and shock, I can make this work.

I put my ear to the door and try to listen to their conversation, but when I hear no voices, I wonder if they're being intimate. An even better compromising position to catch them in, and a motivator to hurt them as much as I can.

Swinging the door open, I step inside the room, my knife raised at my shoulder, ready to use. I lower it immediately when I see them on the stained bed.

Owen, his eyes wide open, stares at the woman beside him. The multiple stab wounds on him are fresh and blood seeps onto the stained mattress. His lifeless body is positioned with his arm over the woman.

I wasn't expecting to see her here.

The receptionist. Alexandria Sutton. The supposed missing woman from my husband's office is lying beside my husband, dead as well. Their bodies are placed to resemble a loving couple about to make love, only they're dead.

On the bare skin of both of them is the mark of their killer. A heart with an X through it. My eyes wide, I nearly scream at the sight. My eyes begin to water as my confusion escalates.

Where's Emma? It was her who said she wanted to meet at the motel.

I look around the small room, my eyes focused on a bloody box cutter on the nightstand beside the bed. The Heartbreak Killer was here tonight. Her latest victims, my husband and his former mistress.

I let out an audible laugh, taking in the irony of the situation. This was my plan. This was how the Heartbreak Killer was going to be caught. Only it was supposed to be Owen.

That's when I look across the room at the other nightstand. Shocked at what I see, I drop my knife, my heart beating out of my chest when I understand what's happening.

My journal. It's here. My name is written on the front of it. I open its pages and see my words. My plan to kill Emma and frame Owen.

A loud bang on the door startles me. "Police! Open the door!" I freeze, but my mind races as I piece together what's happened.

"Open the door!" the officer outside shouts.

It hits me. I've been framed.

CHAPTER 47

Emma

All I ever wanted was to be happy. That's it. I never asked for what happened to me or what I felt I had to do.

As I sit in my car and watch the people around me at the park, I reflect on everything. It's easy to do while listening to an AM radio station that's talking about the breaking news of the return of the Heartbreak Killer. The media has been on an HBK coverage frenzy since the pair of bodies were found in a rundown motel days ago and a woman was arrested.

"The Heartbreak Killer is exactly where she belongs," a criminologist says over the radio. "And did I not tell you all it was a woman?"

"Is she really the Heartbreak Killer though?" the radio host asks. "Some are suggesting it's a copycat killer. After all, the usual MO wasn't used. No duct tape was used to bind the victims and usually a single slit across the throat was performed. We don't know much yet, but authorities have confirmed it was more than just one wound."

The criminologist guest laughs. "Well, the same symbol was found on their bodies. A heart with an X through it. Made, no less, with a box cutter which was found at the crime scene. And as for the reason these murders were different, well, there's a perfectly reasonable explanation. This time it was personal. The victims were the husband of the Heartbreak Killer and his mistress."

"Excellent point," the host says. "The city wondered when we would see the return of the Heartbreak Killer, and we now have our answer. What are your thoughts on why it's been five years since her last murder?"

"Easy," the criminologist says. "Love. Her marriage with her husband, Owen Pearson, occurred near the time of the last known murder of the Heartbreak Killer. Karen Pearson, or, HBK, as we can now call her, was in love. Her cheating husband brought back her dark side."

"Some viewers are still not sold that Karen Pearson is the real serial killer. Have you heard the rumors that a personal journal of Karen's was found at the crime scene?"

I change the channel to a music station that plays classic rock. Queen's *We Are The Champions* is already playing, and I'm tempted to lower the window and blast it. But that would make me trying my best not to be noticeable more difficult.

I smile as I look at a grandpa playing with his grandchild in the nearby playground. Despite all the terrible things that are happening in their lives, they have each other. After I found out the type of person Karen Pearson was, Chloe is better off.

I never wanted the Heartbreak Killer to return. After my last kill, I even started going to AA meetings as a way to keep myself in check. Keep the urges of wanting to fix the broken world around me at bay.

People assume that the Heartbreak Killer murdered out of jealousy or a bad relationship. Due to such a widespread belief, the authorities never looked in my direction. Most of the people I killed, I didn't know well.

What I did know was that the world would be better off without my victims in it.

My first kill was my own father. It took time and skill in using the internet for me to track my dad. When I did, I didn't have bad intentions. I was eighteen and wanted answers.

Why did he leave us after Mom tried to kill him? She was in jail. It wasn't Julie or I who tried to murder him. It was Mom. We needed him when we were kids.

I also wanted to give him back his steel tool kit. When I was a kid, I enjoyed watching him fix things around the house. It was usually the only time he was patient with me. I'd hand him whatever tool he asked for as I watched.

He left most of his belongings in the house after he left us, taking mostly his clothes.

When I found out where he lived, I brought back his precious tools. It was a peace offering. At least at first.

When I spoke with him, he was drunk and belligerent. Told me I was worthless. He was glad Mom was dead.

Out of built-up rage and frustration, I opened the steel box, taking out the rusty box cutter. He was too drunk to fight back.

Working in a rural area, it was actually quite easy for me to hide his body where someone wouldn't find him. Before leaving him at his final resting place, I carved on my first victim what became a symbol of infamy. A heart with an X through it.

Media and the authorities felt it was because I was some heartbroken lover. When it came to my father, I was truly heartbroken, but that's not why I marked his body that way.

I wanted anybody who found him to know that my father had no heart.

It was the same reason why I carved the symbol in the others. My second victim, a man who I worked with briefly at a nightclub downtown, was a misogynist rapist. One night, when he had too much to drink at the club, he talked openly about molesting drunk women at the bar and getting away with it. He thought he was so cool how he used drunk women's bodies for his own pleasure. Some of my male colleagues at the bar thought that was awesome, somehow.

Not me.

There was a problem, and I needed to fix it, because nobody else was willing to. They found his body in the alley near the nightclub. Before leaving him, I pulled down his jeans and boxer shorts, exposing him to the world.

My need to bring justice to those who got away with crimes doesn't limit itself to just men. Women can be just as terrible.

Melissa Santra was someone I met when I was a waitress at a steakhouse. She was in her late thirties when I worked with her. She had a son, who must have been ten when I first met him. Every so often, he'd come to the restaurant after school. He'd do his homework in the back office as his mom and I waited on tables.

I never really liked Melissa much. She always carried a nasty tone and was quick to put others down, including me. But her son was sweet. There was a kindness in him that was plain for anybody to see.

He was a quiet boy. Not very social. At first, I was concerned when he came into the restaurant with a bruised face. A few days later, it was a black eye.

I assumed it was his father. I was wrong.

After work, I tried to get my coworker to confirm for me that it was her husband who was hurting her son. I was going to solve her problem for her. To my surprise, she admitted it was her.

I backed off for a while. When I quit that job, I kept tabs on her son. One day, when I was near their house, I saw him using crutches. A large cast was on his right leg.

That was all the motivation I needed to make my next kill. She would never touch her son again.

All of my victims were heartless people. They each deserved what they got.

But it took a toll on me. I felt I was losing myself in my battle to bring justice to a merciless world where so much wrong goes unpunished. I was only one woman. How much could I do? I would scour articles online, getting angry with all the injustice happening around me in the city.

I decided to make a change. I moved into the country with my sister, her husband and my nephew. It helped. I stopped watching the news and avoided social media like the plague.

I had to stop. Any time that I messed up, read something upsetting, or discovered something terrible happening in my small community, I'd go to an AA meeting.

I don't even like drinking. I'll have maybe one drink a week, if that. Julie was surprised when I told her about my addiction and going to meetings.

But my addiction was murder. I got high when I felt I helped others.

I never meant for the Heartbreak Killer to come back. After Alexandria cornered me by the river and Owen told me the truth about his wife, I admit I was curious. I wasn't planning to kill anyone though.

Alexandria's murder was self-defence. After breaking up with Owen at the motel, I went back. I wish I hadn't, but I did. I saw Alexandria leave the motel room. I was confused. Owen had told me how much he loved me and wanted to keep me safe from his crazy ex-girlfriend, and yet, she was at the motel.

Even from far away, I could make out her bruised face and bloody nose as she hurried to her car. That's when I approached her. I just wanted to tell her the truth. Owen is a terrible man. I wanted to ask her if it was him who did that to her face.

She attacked me. Striking me in the chest and taking out a knife she concealed in her purse. Maybe it was just instinct, but I quickly took out my pocketknife and, without much thought, killed her. I didn't want that.

I hid her body in my trunk, looking around at the empty street, thankful that nobody saw us. She was parked far enough from Owen's room that he didn't seem to hear the noise we made either. I'd come back later to move her vehicle.

As I stuffed her in the back of my trunk, Owen left his room. I followed him all the way to his house while trying to clean Alexandria's blood from my hands and face.

All I wanted to know from Alexandria was if it was Owen who hurt her. Why was she in the motel room? Had Owen told her to come? Did he beat her?

I had many questions, and in a fit of rage, I followed him all the way to his house. I was going to ask him those questions myself, now that it was impossible for Alexandria to speak. That was where I discovered who his wife really was. Karen. The woman who pretended to be friendly with me in an attempt to murder me.

One of the many skills I developed during my

time as the Heartbreak Killer was breaking into houses without being noticed. It wasn't difficult to get into Owen's house or Karen's office. I watched her one night writing in a journal with her name on it. After concluding that it was her who unlocked my bathroom window, I needed to know more.

I got exactly what I needed when I read her journal.

She was going to kill me. Not only that, but she was also going to frame Owen for it. She actually wanted to kill me in the fashion the Heartbreak Killer would have.

The irony was too much for me. I had to repay the favor.

I lower my head as I watch Chloe in the playground being swung by Karen's dad. If it wasn't for that little girl, I would have killed Karen too. The criminologist on the radio was right about the last victims of the Heartbreak Killer. It was personal.

Alexandria's death was self-defence. Owen, well, who's going to miss that lying, cheating, woman-beater? Karen, my final victim, she'll get to stay a long time behind bars playing out the final result she had planned for her husband.

Just as she noted in her journal, people will question if Karen was the real Heartbreak Killer or a copycat. But they won't question if she's a murderer.

I take a deep breath. I know what I've done is wrong, even if in my head, justice was served. There's plenty more injustice in the world though. But I don't have to be the one who fixes the problems any longer.

With Karen behind bars, the Heartbreak Killer can retire.

Beside me on the passenger seat is my dad's steel toolbox. I look outside the window and notice a large dumpster. Without a second thought, I get out of my car and grab the toolbox. I walk up to the dumpster, holding the box to my chest for a moment. I empty the toolbox, letting all the other possible weapons the Heartbreak Killer could have used on new victims fall, dropping the empty steel box in last.

Looking back at the playground, I hurry back to my car and get inside when I see Chloe and her grandfather coming back to the parking lot.

This was a moment I didn't want to miss but also didn't want to get caught watching.

Chloe holds her grandpa's hand as the two stroll towards his car. When they're close enough for her to see what I've left, she points.

"Is that a present?" Chloe shouts, pointing at the thin, wrapped box with a red bowtie placed on the hood of his car. Even with my window rolled up, I can hear how excited she is.

Grandpa looks at his car, confused. I try to conceal myself in my seat and quietly lower my window to listen better.

"Did you get me a toy?" Chloe asks.

"No, I didn't," Grandpa says, puzzled. Chloe runs up to his car and grabs the present, tearing into the paper. "Chloe, that's not ours. I don't know who's that—"

"Grandpa!" she shouts, seeing the toy. "It's the Barbie I wanted. The one with a unicorn horn!" She tightly wraps her small arms around his legs, thanking him profusely.

Grandpa grabs the box and looks at the Barbie doll, a smirk on his face. "I don't think this is yours." He turns the box around and sees the large C that I wrote on the box with a marker.

"Please, Grandpa!" she says. "Can I keep it!"

Her grandpa lowers his hand slowly and hands her the box. "I suppose." He looks around the parking lot but doesn't notice me.

I smile as I watch him put Chloe in her kid's seat in the back, promising her ice cream when they get back home. Chloe doesn't respond though. She's too infatuated, staring at the Barbie doll that she's holding in front of her. I always knew how to pick good presents. It's because I listen to what people want. I listen when they feel nobody else is.

Chloe and her grandpa leave the park and turn onto the street. I take a moment before doing the same, only I go the opposite way.

CHAPTER 48

Karen

"I'm innocent!" I shout through the jail phone at my lawyer, who tells me again to lower my voice. If the glass between us wasn't there, I'd shake him profusely until he understood the truth. Ronald Edgers, a court-appointed lawyer, isn't believing a word I say. The correctional officer comes up to me and says if I can't remain calm, the visit from my lawyer will end.

I apologize to my lawyer and the officer. The guard steps back to the edge of the room, monitoring me closely.

I look at my lawyer, pleading with him at an appropriate sound level to understand. "I didn't kill my husband. I didn't kill Alexandria. It was Emma."

He shakes his head. "We have to present to the judge our case and your plea of guilty or not guilty, Karen."

"The answer is easy," I say, trying my best to stay calm through gritted teeth. "It was Emma. She did this. She's the Heartbreak Killer, not me."

"Emma who?" the lawyer says with a tone. It's one

he's given me in the past. He scoffs. "You don't know her last name. You want me to defend you, saying your husband's mistress is the Heartbreak Killer, but you don't even have a last name for me to use?"

I lower my head. "I know where she lives though," I say again. It's a losing argument, but it needs to be repeated.

"You've told me this," he says. "The landlord did describe a woman named Emma. The woman paid in cash. She lived in an area where people kept to themselves. Nobody knew her."

I raise my hands in disgust, and the guard gives me a look. I whisper sorry to him and try my best to contain my antics. It's hard when you're being framed. "Didn't you get her number from Owen's phone records?"

He nods. "We did, but nothing's changed from the last time you said this. The number was created under a fake name. It's a cell phone that works with paid minutes. It's what we call a burner phone. It's complicated to find out information on phones like this."

I shake my head, trying my best not to yell at my stupid lawyer. "Well, isn't that suspicious?"

He agrees. It seems I'm finally reaching him. "The police don't really care about this woman," he says. "They're looking for her, but as far as they're concerned, they caught the killer." He points a finger against the glass. "You."

I shake my head in disbelief. "Ron, you have to believe me."

He lowers his head. "This is an ironclad case, Karen. You were at the crime scene when police arrived. Your journal was found at the location. Those were your words, were they not? The ones that described killing your husband's girlfriend?"

"Those were my words," I admit. "But I didn't kill Alexandria. I didn't murder Owen."

He takes a deep breath, looking at his watch. "And yet, in your journal, you described killing him." He shakes his head. "Do you not understand how this looks?"

I put my hand on the window. "I'm not the Heartbreak Killer."

He nods. "The police don't think you are either. A copycat, though. I mean, you wrote out the plan in your journal."

"I'm not guilty," I say. "I won't plead guilty for something I didn't do."

"The Crown Prosecutor has testimony from some teenaged cashier at a home hardware store that remembers you buying a box cutter and duct tape with your daughter days before the double murder."

"I didn't do it, Ron. I didn't kill them. That box cutter I bought was brand new. The one they found was old and rusty. Don't you see?"

He sighs again. "This is a losing battle, Karen. You get that, right? If you don't accept a plea, you'll be in jail for a lot longer. There is no way to win this case." He clears his throat. "Listen, you have a young daughter. Your dad has custody right now, but if you ever want to see her before she turns forty, do yourself a favor, take the plea deal."

"I can't do that!" I shout. The correctional officer demands that I lower my voice again. I ignore him. "It was Emma! She's the Heartbreak Killer!"

EPILOGUE

Emma

Julie catches my attention from the dance floor, waving for me to join her and David. I smile and shake my head. She gestures more aggressively for me to participate in the line dancing group as they do their choreographed moves to the beat of some old country music song.

I have no clue what they're doing or how they're doing it. No thanks. I pretend to cover my face, and when I look, she's smiling back, resuming her dance, her husband beside her.

Even though it hasn't been too long since I've moved back to my sister's house, I feel better out here. Life is slower, and I'm okay with that, for now.

I reluctantly took a job as a receptionist at my brother-in-law's chiropractic clinic. When taking the position, I was forced to agree to no "you're not a doctor" remarks while on the clock. When I'm not working, however, there are no limits to our banter.

I smile, watching my sister's husband tilt his

white cowboy hat to Julie as he swoops in and dips her unexpectedly. I laugh as the two nearly fall, their several drinks contributing to his lack of smoothness on the dance floor.

Taking a sip of my coke, with no liquor in it for appearance's sake, I notice it's nearly all gone. I look at the bar to see how empty it is. Only a pair of men catch my attention. One of them, a man I know as Steve, smiles at me.

Steve's an idiot. He's spoken to me in the past. Attempted to hit on me in this bar over a year ago. I let him down gently.

His friend, however, he's new and very handsome. He turns to look at me as Steve gawks in my direction. The mystery man looks even more handsome as our eyes meet. He reminds me of a young Channing Tatum. His light green eyes narrow on me and I quickly look away. When I turn back, he smiles as he turns to his friend.

I take a deep breath. It's been months since I moved back to Julie's house. She was more than willing to open her house to me again. I had one request, though. I can't go back to the basement. I need sunlight in my life so as to not feel like a troll underneath them.

I have to admit, I'm happy being back in this small town. As much as I enjoy spending time with Julie and my nephew, I'm saving up for my own place. Another month or two, and I'll be ready to move out. Julie insisted that I take my time with the move.

After what happened when I returned to Windsor, I thought I'd have a hard time with my dark thoughts.

Julie insisted that I go back to my AA meetings, but I've been fine.

No bad urges. A slow life, where problems don't seem to come my way like they do in the city. I feel like small town living suits me better. When I'm in the city, I'm surrounded by society's trauma. Here, I'm surrounded by the people in this world who love me.

"Excuse me," a deep voice says. I turn and it's Channing Tatum again, only now he's at my table. He smiles at me as our eyes meet again. I can feel myself melt in his gaze. "My name's Jackson." He extends his hand.

"I'm Emma," I say, taking it. His grip is tight, but I can tell he's trying to be delicate.

"Can I sit with you?" he asks.

I'm taken back by his politeness. I was already gushing over his looks, but now gritty Channing Tatum has my full attention. Julie's too, I notice as I look over his shoulder and see her smiling at me as she whispers something in David's ear.

"Sure," I say, trying to not come off too excited. Just looking at this man, I can tell he's trouble. He may be polite, but his eyes are already undressing me. But he also seems like the type to want to get to know me after. The kind of man who has a high probability of bringing loads of unnecessary baggage into my life. A person who has a bunch of flaws, but because of his charms and good looks, I'm willing to overlook them. After all, I can *fix* him.

"So," Jackson says, sitting across from me, "tell me about yourself, Emma." He brandishes another devilish smile, and already I'm infatuated with him.

I take my last sip of my coke and smile. Dating was not on my mind when I came back to this small town.

But I'll never give up on love.

* * *

Note from the author:

I truly hope you enjoyed reading my story as much as I did creating it. As an indie author, what you think of my book is all I care about.

If you enjoyed my story, please take a moment to leave your review on Amazon. It would mean the world to me.

Thank you for reading, and I hope you join me next time.

Sincerely,
James

Download My Free Book

If you would like to receive a FREE copy of my psychological thriller, The Affair, email me at jamescaineauthor@gmail.com.

I'm always happy to hear from readers.

Thanks again,
James

Now, please enjoy a sample of my book, Keep the Doctor Away:

PROLOGUE

"Lily," a soft voice says to me. My body is gently pushed. "Wake up, darling. You must wake up now."

I attempt to open my eyes, and when I do, Mommy is staring at me, concerned.

"Mom?" I say, confused when I notice it's still dark outside. "What time is it?" I start to yawn. I didn't sleep for too long.

Mommy says I sleep too much for a little girl who just turned seven last week. She tells me that I'm already sleeping like a teenager.

"Lily," she whispers aggressively. "Look at me."

I blink several times, attempting to understand why she's upset. "Mom, is—"

She puts a finger to my lip and looks around my bedroom. "You must be quiet, dear." She extends her hand to me. "We have to leave. They're here."

As she speaks, I'm more and more awake to the point where her words begin to scare me. The look on Mommy's face scares me more. Her eyes are wide but dull. Her usual loving stare is nonexistent.

"Who's here, Mom?" I whisper back, scared of what she's about to say. I've seen *Home Alone* with her. Mommy told me about the bad people who live in the world. People who do bad things to others and try and get away with it.

Those who kidnap children, hurt people and steal candy.

She puts another finger to her mouth and raises her eyebrows, shushing me. "We can't let them know where we are, Lily. They'll take you if they know."

"Take me?" I say, my expression matching hers now. "Who?"

She doesn't say. Instead, she puts out her hand and I grab it. I quietly get out of bed as she guides me out of my room. She reminds me again to be quiet as we walk down the hallway.

Echoed sounds of the television coming from Mommy and Daddy's room play along the hall. Daddy's watching the news late tonight. The reporter is speaking of a double homicide in Edmonton.

Mommy's face becomes more stern as we get near her bedroom. "You must close your eyes, Lily," she tells me. "Your father is one of *them*."

"Daddy?" I say confused.

"He was one of them, Lily. He wanted to hurt you. He can't any longer. I made sure of it. Now, close your eyes," she demands in her whispered tone.

I do as Mommy asks as we get closer to Daddy in the bedroom. As Mommy guides me along the hallway, I keep my eyelids shut, listening to the sound of the news reporter speaking of a terrible crime that happened.

"A murder suicide has been confirmed in a condo in the Whitemud area tonight. Two people dead. A young child was found unharmed."

I make a mistake and open my eyes to see the television. Instead, I see Daddy laying on the bed. His white button-up shirt he had on for dinner is stained red, and he's sleeping. Only I don't hear him snoring loudly as he usually does.

"Close your eyes, now!" Mom shouts.

I immediately shut them again. I can't stop thinking of Daddy and his stained shirt. We didn't have spaghetti or anything that could dirty his shirt for dinner. Daddy always makes fun of me for eating like a "piggy" and getting myself all dirty.

I realize that Daddy may be hurt.

Mom pulls on my arm, but I shrug her off and open my eyes again. "Daddy!" I shout.

Mom lowers to my side and quickly covers my mouth. Tears well in my eyes and drip down my cheeks, going between her fingers. Her hand is forceful over my lips as she looks around frantically.

"Quiet, Lily," she whispers in my ear. "They'll come for us next."

Mom turns her head quickly behind her as if something is there. When I look, there's no one. Suddenly she looks at the walls and stands up. She shoves me directly behind her and stands between me and the empty hall.

"You can't have her!" Mommy shouts. "I won't let you take her! You'll have to take me first!"

"I'm scared," I cry out. I look over at my father and I know that he's dead.

"You will not take my daughter!" Mommy shouts at the narrow hallway. She stares blankly at one wall. "No!" she screams. She kicks into the wall, leaving a mark in the plaster.

"Mommy!" I shriek. "What's happening?"

"Don't you see!" she says, turning to me. "Don't you see their eyes? They're everywhere! They'll come for you! I won't let them have you." Mom turns to the other side of the wall and kicks again, making an even larger dent.

A loud knock on the front door downstairs catches both of our attention.

"They're here!" Mommy shouts. "They've come for you, Lily." I run downstairs, my mother's words chasing me. "What are you doing?" she screams. "They're here! Lily!"

When I open the door, a police officer looks at me like I'm a ghost. I run up to his legs, hugging them tightly.

"Lily!" Mom shouts from upstairs. "They'll come for you! Don't let them take you! They'll never let you go!"

The officer's eyes are wide as he watches my mother raving at the top of the stairs. He gently guides me behind him and takes out his gun.

CHAPTER 1

It starts to rain as the boat carries us across the lake to an area known as Northwind Island.

They say rain on an important day is an omen. I don't exactly believe in omens, but if I did, I'd be really worried. What starts as a few drops turns quickly into a torrential downpour.

David wipes his face and shouts at the pilot of the boat if we should turn around, back to the mainland, as we get soaked. The pilot shakes his head, saying we're more than halfway to the island now. It's best to continue.

David grabs my hand tightly as he sits down. "He says we need to keep going to the island."

"I'm wet from head to toe," I yell, but with the heavy rain and sound of the boat racing across the water, he doesn't hear me. I shout it again and this time he does.

"We just have to put up with it, Lily," my husband says.

As the ride continues, and the rain shows no sign of slowing, I can see the nervousness in David's eyes as he looks out over the lake. Northwind is in sight now. The pilot lets us know we only have a few minutes before we dock. With the weather turning worse, I'm thankful for it.

Northwind Island. My new home. Our new home.

In the distance, I see a tall white wall. Peeking over the top is a row of houses. David told me that we would be living in a house for free while we stayed on the island. I imagine one of the luxurious houses I see now could be ours.

I remember how happy David looked when he got the call from his old mentor, Dr. Keenan, offering him a position as a surgeon at his private clinic.

David felt it was his "big break", as he kept calling it. Life as a surgeon was not going how he hoped it would.

After four years of an undergraduate degree at the University of Edmonton, finishing four additional years in med school and finally, five more years in a surgical residency, he thought he would have it made. But instead of the riches he had promised me before we got married, all we had was a student debt that would be anyone's worst nightmare and a lot more debt from him not working.

I had been employed at a call center working as a customer service representative. I'd have to work until retirement to pay off the amount of money David owed from his quest to become a surgeon.

"Don't worry about it, Lily," he'd tell me. "Once I'm a surgeon, the big bucks will come, and everything will be paid off. We'll have one of those dream homes you see in magazines. The lifestyle that will change the future not only our lives but our future kids', and possibly theirs."

None of that mattered to me. Most of the time it was David who brought up his money concerns or fantasies about how much he'd make and he'd go on and on about how everything would be okay.

I'm not sure if he was trying to reassure himself more than me.

Like me, David's parents were poor, less than poor even. Despite his father having two jobs, he was not able to keep up with bills, mostly due to his drinking and gambling problems.

He never got along with his father. It's been years since he spoke to him.

David was an oversharer and would tell me many terrible stories about what living in his house was like growing up. He couldn't wait to move out and immediately after turning eighteen, he did. He worked hard to get as much as he could from scholarships for school.

Because of his determination, I knew we would be okay financially. David had always wanted to save people's lives with his hands. He was obsessed with the idea of him being able to help others. He had little interest in being a regular physician because of it.

After he finished his residency, though, he couldn't find work. All those years of school and residency were washed down the drain... I couldn't understand how.

Didn't the country need more surgeons? Wasn't it a speciality that always needed new blood?

After eight months of being unemployed and finding work where he could, David got his "big break". Dr. Keenan, one of the surgeons he worked closely with during his residency, called him and offered him a dream job. One that David would have to be crazy not to accept.

Be a plastic surgeon at a private clinic on an island. What kind of a set up was this? David told me in advance the wealth the patrons in the clinic had to be able to go there. Of course, he wasn't supposed to. He wasn't supposed to tell anyone. Both of us had to sign a non-disclosure agreement before he was officially hired.

THE CHEATING HUSBAND

A private plastic surgery clinic on an island for the wealthy.

David had told me that there were celebrities that visited the clinic as well. Staff were sworn to secrecy. Hollywood had a way of shaming celebrities if it became known that they had some work done.

For whatever reason, society expects the beautiful to stay beautiful, but without any intervention, especially of the surgical kind.

For that reason, use of cellphones, internet and any social media was prohibited. Staff lived on the island and were expected to keep everything they saw there to themselves.

As the boat gets closer and I start to see the tall white walls surrounding the clinic, I wonder just what I have got myself into.

To my surprise, the rainfall begins to ease. It seems the storm waited for us to be stuck on a boat before drowning us from the sky. Of course, now that we're almost at the island, the rain stops.

David appears even more uneasy. He's shivering from being soaking wet, and so am I, but he's doing that thing he does with his hands when he's nervous. He clamps them together, fidgeting his thumbs around.

He was like this last night as well in the hotel room. We weren't able to get a boat ride until early the next day so we spent the night on the mainland. Usually, David's an early sleeper. He's knocked out by nine most days. Yesterday, though, as my eyes began to shut, he was wide eyed, staring off at the dated wallpaper of the hotel room.

At one point when I woke up, I saw David staring at a picture of his old house. It was the one he was raised in. The one he left at eighteen. He keeps a beat-up picture of it in his wallet. At times when he's nervous, he takes it out. I've seen him do it before.

He told me he looked at the photo to remind himself of the nightmare he grew up in and how hard he worked to ensure he wouldn't have the same life he had as a child. Somehow looking at that house gives him comfort.

I don't understand it myself.

I never talk about my past. I keep that to myself. I don't keep pictures of my family home like David. The idea would be too painful.

David has monsters in his past with his father, but I still have nightmares of my mother that night when I was taken away from her.

I'm fine with the past staying there. The future is ahead of me, and for now that's on Northwind Island. Now it's David's time to find happiness in a job he imagined doing his whole life.

I was less than happy with the idea of living on a secluded island. David told me many people lived there, though. I didn't like the idea of leaving the small group of friends we had back in Edmonton. David told me I'd make new ones.

"If it doesn't work out, Lily," he told me, "we could leave in a few years and I'd have many jobs lined up for me at that point. We could buy a huge house. Finally start our family. Live the life others only dream about. Or, who knows, maybe we'll love it on the island and stay."

Northwind Island is a small island located in northern Ontario. It's only accessible by boat. Its shoreline is a mix of rocky edges and sandy beaches. I grin as we get closer to our new home.

The pilot slows down as we get closer to a long dock. He stops the engine completely and quickly ties the boat up. He steps off and onto the dock. He smiles as he extends a hand to me.

I thank him as I take his hand and step onto the dock. My husband steps off next to me. We are completely soaked. I worry how wet our clothes in our bags are.

"Welcome to Northwind Island," the pilot says to us.

Printed in Dunstable, United Kingdom